Richard Doddridge Blackmore

Fringilla

Some tales in verse

Richard Doddridge Blackmore

Fringilla
Some tales in verse

ISBN/EAN: 9783337174071

Printed in Europe, USA, Canada, Australia, Japan

Cover: Foto ©Andreas Hilbeck / pixelio.de

More available books at **www.hansebooks.com**

FRINGILLA

SOME·TALES·IN·VERSE
By RICHARD DODDRIDGE
BLACKMORE
PICTVRED·BY LOVIS·
FAIRFAX-MVCKLEY
WITH·III·DRAWINGS·
BY·JAMES LINTON

Quorsum haec? Non potui qualem
Philomela querelam; sed
fringilla velut pipitabunda vagor.

LONDON·PVBLISHED
By ELKIN·MATHEWS
IN·VIGO·STREET
MDCCCXCV

PREFACE

[*Fringilla loquitur*]

"What means your finch?" "Being well aware that he cannot sing like a Nightingale,
He flits about from tree to tree, and twitters a little tale."

ALBEIT he is an ancient bird, who tried his pipe in better days, and then was scared by random shots, he is fain to lift the migrant wing once more towards the humble perch, among the trees he loves. All gardeners own that he does no harm, unless he flits into a thicket of young buds, or a very choice ladies' seed-bed. And he hopes that he is now too wise to commit such indiscretions.

Perhaps it would have been wiser still to have shut up his little mandible, or employed it only upon grub. But the long gnaw of last winter's frost, which set mankind a-shivering, even in their most downy nest, has made them kindly to the race that has no roof for shelter and no hearth for warmth.

Anyhow, this little finch can do no harm, if he does no good; and if he pleases nobody, he will not be surprised, because he has never satisfied himself.

May-day, 1895.

NOTE

With kind consent of Messrs. Harper, " Buscombe " returns in altered form from the other side of the ocean. Two other little tales appeared of old, but nobody would look at them, and now they are offered after careful trimming.

Standing afar, I gaze with doubt at other trimmings which are not mine. They have conquered the taste of the day perhaps, and high art announces them as her last transfiguration. Moreover they are highly recommended—as the purest art not always is—by the modesty of the artist.

R. D. B.

THE TABLE OF CONTENTS

◂❡ The cover design, borders, initial letters, and the whole of the full-page illustrations—with the exception of the three to ' Pausias and Glycera' by James W. R. Linton—are by Louis Fairfax-Muckley.

I

HOU feeble implement of mind,
　Wherewith she strove to scrawl her
　　name;
But, like a mitcher, left behind
　No signature, no stroke, no claim,
　No hint that she hath pined—

Shall ever come a stronger time,
　When thou shalt be a tool of skill,
　And steadfast purpose, to fulfil
A higher task than rhyme?

II

Thou puny instrument of soul,
　Wherewith she labours to impart
Her efforts at some arduous goal;
　But fails to bring thy coarser art
　Beneath a fine control—

Shall ever come a fairer day,
　When thou shalt be a buoyant plume,
　To soar, where clearer suns illume,
And fresher breezes play?

III

Thou weak interpreter of heart,
  So impotent to tell the tale
Of love's delight, of envy's smart,
  Of passion, and ambition's bale,
  Of pride that dwells apart—

Shall I, in length of time, attain
  (By walking in the human ways,
  With love of Him, who made and sways
To ply thee, less in vain?

IV

If so, thou shalt be more to me
  Than sword, or sceptre, flag, or crown ;
With mind, and soul, and heart in thee,
  Despising gold, and sham renown ;
  But truthful, kind, and free.

Then come ; though now a pithless quill,
  Uncouth, unfledged, indefinite,—
  In time, thou shalt be taught to write,
By patience, and good-will.

1854.

LITA OF THE NILE
A TALE IN THREE PARTS
PART I

I

"KING, and Father, gift and giver,
God revealed in form of river,
Issuing perfect, and sublime,
From the fountain-head of time;

"Whom eternal mystery
    shroudeth,
Unapproached, untracked, unknown;
Whom the Lord of heaven encloudeth
  With the curtains of His throne;

"From the throne of heaven descending,
Glory, power, and goodness blending,
Grant us, ere the daylight dies,
Token of thy rapid rise."

II

Ha, it cometh! Furrowing, flashing,
    Red blood rushing o'er brown breast;
Peaks, and ridges, and domes, dashing
    Foam on foam, and crest on crest!

'Tis the signal Thebes hath waited,
Libyan Thebes, the hundred-gated:
Rouse, and robe thee, River-priest
For thy dedication feast!

Follows him the loveliest maiden,
    Afric's thousand hills can show;
White apparel'd, flower-laden,
    With the lotus on her brow.

III

Votive maid, who hath espousal
Of the river's high carousal;
Twenty cubits if he rise,
This shall be his bridal prize.

Calm, and meek of face and carriage,
    Deigning scarce a quicker breath,
Comes she to the funeral marriage,
    The betrothal of black death.

Rosy hands, and hennaed fingers,
Nails whereon the onyx lingers,
Clasped, as at a lover's tale,
In the bosom's marble vale.

IV

Silvery scarf, her waist enwreathing,
　Wafts a soft Sabæan balm ;
Like a cloud of incense, breathing
　Round the column of a palm :

Snood of lilies interweaveth
(Giving less than it receiveth)
Beauty of her cluster'd brow,
Calmly bent upon us now.

Through her dark hair, spread before us,
　See the western glory wane,
As in groves of dim Cytorus,
　Or the bowers of Taprobane !

V

See, the large eyes, lit by heaven,
Brighter than the Sisters Seven,
(Like a star the storm hath cowed)
Sink their flash in sorrow's cloud.

There the crystal tear refraineth,
　And the founts of grief are dry ;
" Father, Mother—none remaineth ;
　All are dead ; and why not I ?"

Yet, by God's will, heavenly beauty
Owes to Heaven alone its duty ;
Off ye priests, who dare adjudge
Bride, like this, to slime and sludge !

7

VI

When they tread the river's margent,
  All their mitred heads are bowed—
What hath browned the ripples argent,
  Like the plume of thunder-cloud?

Where yestreen the water slumbered,
With a sickly crust encumbered,
Leapeth now a roaring flood,
Wild as war, and red as blood.

Every billow hurries quicker,
  Every surge runs up the strand ;
While the brindled eddies flicker,
  Scourged as with a levin brand.

VII

Every bulrush, parched and welted,
Lifts his long joints yellow-belted ;
Every lotus, faint and sick,
Hangs her fragrant tongue to lick.

Countless creatures, long unthought of,
  Swarm from every hole and nook ;
What is man, that he make nought of
  Other entries in God's book?

Scorpions, rats, and lizards flabby,
Centipedes, and hydras scabby,
Asp, and slug, and toad, whose gem
Outlasts human diadem.

8

VIII

Therefore hath the priest-procession
  Causeway clean of sandal-wood ;
That no foul thing make transgression
  On the votive maiden's blood.

Pure of blood and soul, she standeth
Where the marble gauge demandeth,
Marble pillar, with black style,
Record of the rising Nile.

White-robed priests around her kneeling,
  Ibis-banner floating high,
Conchs, and drums, and sistrals pealing,
  And Sesostris standing nigh.

IX

He, whose kingdom-city stretches
Further than our eyesight fetches ;
Every street it wanders down
Larger than a regal town ;

Built, when each man was a giant,
  When the rocks were mason's stones,
When the oaks were osiers pliant,
  And the mountains scarcely thrones ;

City, whose Titanic portals
Scorn the puny modern mortals,
In thy desert winding-sheet,
Sacred from our insect feet.

X

Thebes No-Amon, hundred-gated,
  Every gate could then unfold
Cavalry ten thousand, plated,
  Man and horse, in solid gold.

Glancing back through serried ranges,
Vivid as his own phalanges,
Every captain might espy
Equal host in sculpture vie;

Down Piromid vista gazing,
  Ten miles back from every gate,
He can see that temple blazing,
  Which the world shall never mate.

XI

But the Nile-flood, when it swelleth,
Recks not man, nor where he dwelleth;
And—e'en while Sesostris reigns—
Scarce five cubits man attains.

Lo, the darkening river quaileth,
  Like a swamp by giant trod,
And the broad commotion waileth,
  Stricken with the hand of God!

When the rushing deluge raging
Flung its flanks, and shook the staging,
Priesthood, cowering from the brim,
Chanted thus its faltering hymn.

XII

"Ocean sire, the earth enclasping,
    Like a babe upon thy knee,
In thy cosmic cycle grasping
    All that hath been, or shall be;

"Thou, that art around and over
All we labour to discover;
Thou, to whom our world no more
Than a shell is on thy shore;

"God, that wast Supreme, or ever
    Orus, or Osiris, saw;
God, with whom is no endeavour,
    But thy will eternal law:

XIII

"We, who keep thy feasts and fastings,
We, who live on thy off-castings,
Here in low obeisance crave
Rich abundance of thy wave.

"Seven years now, for some transgression,
    Some neglect, or outrage vile,
Vainly hath our poor procession
    Offered life, and soul to Nile.

"Seven years now of promise fickle,
Niggard ooze, and paltry trickle,
Freshet sprinkling scanty dole,
Where the roaring flood should roll.

11

XIV

" Therefore are thy children dwindled,
Therefore is thine altar bare ;
Wheat, and rye, and millet spindled,
And the fruits of earth despair.

" Men with haggard bellies languish,
Bridal beds are strewn with anguish,
Mothers sell their babes for bread,
Half the holy kine are dead.

" Is thy wrath at last relaxing ?
Art thou merciful, once more ?
Yea, behold the torrent waxing !
Yea, behold the flooded shore !

XV

" Nile, that now with life-blood tidest,
And in gorgeous gold subsidest,
Richer than our victor tread
Stirred in far Hydaspes' bed;

" When thy swelling crest o'er-waveth
Yonder twenty cubit mark,
And thy tongue of white foam laveth
Borders of the desert dark,

" This, the fairest Theban maiden,
Shall be thine, with jewels laden ;
Lift thy furrowed brow, and see
Lita, dedicate to thee ! "

12

XVI

Thus he spake, and lowly stooping
  O'er the Calasiris hem,
Took the holy water, scooping
  With a bowl of lucid gem ;

Chanting from the Bybline psalter
Touched he then her forehead altar ;
Sleeking back the trickled jet,
There the marriage-seal he set.

" None of mortals dare pursue thee,
    None come near thy hallowed side :
Nile's thou art, and he shall woo thee,—
    Nile, who swalloweth his bride."

XVII

With despair's mute self-reliance,
She accepted death's affiance ;
She, who hath no home or rest,
Shrank not from the river's breast.

Haply there she shall discover
  Father, lost in wilds unknown,
Mother slain, and youthful lover,
  Seen as yet in dreams alone.

Ha! sweet maid, what sudden vision
Hath dispelled thy cold derision ?
What new picture hast thou seen,
Of a world that might have been ?

XVIII

From Mount Seir, Duke Iram roveth,
  Three renewals of the moon :
To see Egypt him behoveth,
  Ere his life be past its noon.

Soul, and mind, at first fell under
Flat discomfiture of wonder,
With the Nile before him spread,
Temple-crowned, and tempest-fed !

Yet a nobler creed he owneth,
  Than to worship things of space :
One true God his heart enthroneth—
Heart that throbs with Esau's race.

XIX

Thus he stood, with calm eyes scorning
Idols, priests, and their adorning ;
Seeing, e'en in nature's show,
Him alone, who made it so.

"God of Abraham, our Father,
  Earth, and heaven, and all we see,
Are but gifts of thine, to gather
  Us, thy children, back to Thee.

"All the grandeur spread before us,
All the miracles shed o'er us,
Echoes of the voice above,
Tokens of a Father's love."

XX

While of heaven his heart indited,
  And his dark eyes swept the crowd,
Sudden on the maid they lighted,
  Mild and haughty, meek and proud.

Rapid as the flash of sabre,
Strong as giant's toss of caber,
Sure as victor's grasp of goal,
Came the love-stroke through his soul.

Gently she, her eyes recalling,
  Felt that Heaven had touched their flight,
Peeped again, through lashes falling,
  Blushed, and shrank, and shunned the light.

XXI

Ah, what booteth sweet illusion,
Fluttering glance, and soft suffusion,
Bliss unknown, but felt in sighs,
Breast, that shrinks at its own rise?

She, who is the Nile's devoted,
  Courted with a watery smile;
Her betrothal duly noted
  By the bridesmaid Crocodile!

So she bowed her forehead lowly,
Tightened her tiara holy;
And, with every sigh suppressed,
Clasped her hands on passion's breast.

PART II

I

TWICE the moon hath waxed and wasted,
　　Lavish of her dew-bright horn;
　　And the wheeling sun hath hasted
Fifty days, towards Capricorn.

Thebes, and all the Misric nation,
Float upon the inundation;
Each man shouts and laughs, before
Landing at his own house door.

There the good wife doth return it,
　　Grumbling, as she shows the dish,
Chervil, basil, chives, and burnet
　　Feed, instead of seasoning, fish.

II

Palm trees, grouped upon the highland,
Here and there make pleasant island;
On the bark some wag hath wrote—
"Who would fly, when he can float?"

Udder'd cows are standing pensive,
　　Not belonging to that ilk;
How shall horn, or tail defensive,
　　Keep the water from their milk?

Lo, the black swan, paddling slowly,
Pintail ducks, and sheldrakes holy,
Nile-goose flaked, and herons gray,
Silver-voiced at fall of day!

III

Flood hath swallowed dikes and hedges,
   Lately by Sesostris planned ;
Till, like ropes, its matted edges
   Quiver on the desert sand.

Then each farmer, brisk and mellow;
Graspeth by the hand his fellow ;
And, as one gone labour-proof,
Shakes his head at the drowned shadoof.

Soon the Nuphar comes, beguiling
   Sedgy spears, and swords around,.
Like that cradled infant smiling,
   Whom the royal maiden found..

IV

But the time of times for wonder
Is when ruddy sun goes under ;
And the dusk throws, half afraid,
Silver shuttles of long shade..

Opens then a scene, the fairest
   Ever burst on human view;
Once behold, and thou comparest
   Nothing in the world thereto..

While the broad flood murmurs glistening
To the moon that hangeth listening—
Moon that looketh down the sky,
Like an aloe-bloom on high—

V

Sudden conch o'er the wave ringeth !
  Ere the date-leaves cease to shake,
All, that hath existence, springeth
  Into broad light, wide-awake.

As at a window of heaven thrown up,
All in a dazzling blaze are shown up,
Mellowing, ere our eyes avail,
To some soft enchanter's tale.

Every skiff a big ship seemeth,
  Every bush with tall wings clad ;
Every man his good brain deemeth
  The only brain that is not mad.

VI

Hark ! The pulse of measured rowing,
And the silver clarions blowing,
From the distant darkness, break
Into this illumined lake.

'Tis Sesostris, lord of nations,
  Victor of three continents,
Visiting the celebrations,
  Priests, and pomps, and regiments.

Kings, from Indus, and Araxes,
Ister, and the Boreal axes,
Horsed his chariot to the waves,
Then embarked, his galley-slaves.

VII

Glittering stands the giant royal,
    Four tall sons are at his back;
Twain, with their own corpses loyal,
    Bridged the flames Pelusiac.

As he passeth, myriads bless him,
Glorious Monarch all confess him,
Sternly upright, to condone
No injustice, save his own.

He, well-pleased, his sceptre swingeth,
    While his four sons strike the gong;
Till the sparkling water ringeth
    Joy and laughter, joke and song.

VIII

Ah, but while loud merry-making
Sets the lights and shadows shaking,
While the mad world casts away
Every thought that is not gay,

Hath not earth, our sweet step-mother,
    Very different scene hard by,
Tossing one, and trampling other,
    Some to laugh, and some to sigh?

Where the fane of Hathor lowereth,
And the black Myrike embowereth,
Weepeth one her life gone by;
Over young, oh death, to die!

IX

Nay, but lately she was yearning
  To be quit of life's turmoil,
In the land of no returning,
  Where all travel ends, and toil.

What temptations now entice her?
What hath made the world seem nicer?
Whence the charm, that strives anew
To prolong this last adieu?

Ah, her heart can understand it,
  Though her tongue can ne'er explain:
Let yon granite Sphinx demand it—
  Riddle, ever solved in vain.

X

No constraint of hands hath bound her,
Not a chain hath e'er been round her;
Silver star hath sealed her brow,
Holy as an Isis cow.

Free to wander where she listeth;
  No immurement must defile
(So the ancient law insisteth)
  This, the hallowed bride of Nile.

What recks Abraham's descendant
Idols, priests, and pomps attendant?
And how long shall nature heed
What the stocks and stones decreed?

22

XI

" Fiendish superstitions hold thee
    To a vile and hideous death.
Break their bonds ; let love enfold thee ;
    Off, and fly with me ; "—he saith.

" Off ! while priests are cutting capers—
Priests of beetles, cats, and tapirs,
Brutes, who would thy beauty truck
For an inch of yellow muck.

" Lo, my horse, *Pyropus*, yearneth
    For the touch of thy light form ;
Like the lightning, his eye burneth ;
    And his nostril, like the storm.

XII

" What are those unholy pagans ?
    Can they ride ? No more than Dagons.
Fishtails ne'er could sit a steed ;
    That belongs to Esau's seed.

" I will make thee Queen of far lands,
    Flocks, and herds, and camel-trains,
Milk and honey, fruit and garlands,
    Vines and venison, woods and wains.

" God is with us ; He shall speed us ;
Or (if this vile crew impede us)
Let some light into their brain,
By the sword of Tubal Cain."

XIII

" Nay," she answered, deeply sighing,
    As the maid grew womanish—
" Love, how hard have I been trying
    To believe the thing I wish !

" Thou hast taught me holy teachings,
    Where to offer my beseechings,
    Homage due to Heaven alone,
    Not to ghosts, and graven stone.

" Thou hast shown me truth and freedom,
    Love, and faith in One most High ;
    But thou hast not, Prince of Edom,
    Taught me therewithal, to lie.

XIV

" Little cause had I for fretting,
    None on earth to be regretting ;
    Till I saw thee, brave and kind ;
    And my heart undid my mind.

" Better, if the Gods had slain me,
    When no difference could be ;
    Ere the joy had come to pain me,
    And, alas, my dear one, thee !

" But shall my poor life throw shame on
    Royal lineage of Amon ?
    'Tis of Egypt's oldest strains ;
    Kingly blood flows in my veins.

24

XV

"Thou hast seen; my faith is plighted,
  That I will not fly my doom.
Honour is a flower unblighted,
  Though the fates cut off its bloom.

"I have sent my last sun sleeping,
  And I am ashamed of weeping.
God, my new God, give me grace
To be worthy of my race.

"Though this death our bodies sever,
  Thou shalt find me there above;
Where I shall be learning ever,
  To be worthy of thy love."

XVI

From his gaze she turned, to borrow
Pride's assistance against sorrow—
God vouchsafes that scanty loan,
When He taketh all our own.

Sudden thought of heaven's inspiring
  Flashed through bold Duke Iram's heart;
Angels more than stand admiring,
  When a man takes his own part.

'Tis the law the Lord hath taught us,
To undo what Satan wrought us;
To confound the foul fiend's plan,
With the manliness of man.

XVII

"Thou art right," he answered lowly,
  As a youth should speak a maid;
"Like thyself, thy word is holy;
  Love is hate, if it degrade.

"But when thou hast well surrendered,
And thy sacrifice is tendered—
God do so, and more to me,
If I slay not, who slay thee!

"Abraham's God hath ne'er forsaken
  Them who trust in Him alway.
Thy sweet life shall not be taken.
  Rest, and calm thee, while I pray."

XVIII

Like a little child, that kneeleth
To tell God whate'er he feeleth,
Bent the tall young warrior there,
And the palm-trees whispered prayer.

She, outworn with woe and weeping,
  Shared that influence from above;
And the fear of death went sleeping
  In the maiden faith and love.

Less the stormy water waileth,
E'en the human tumult faileth;
Stars their silent torches light,
To conduct the car of night.

PART III

I

L O, how bright-eyed morn awaketh
  Tower and temple, nook and Nile;
  How the sun exultant maketh
All the world return his smile!

O'er the dry sand, vapour twinkleth,
Like an eye when old age wrinkleth;
While, along the watered shore
Runs a river of gold ore.

Temple-front and court resemble
  Mirrors swung in wavering light;
While the tapering columns tremble
  At the view of their own height.

II

Marble shaft, and granite portal,
Statues of the Gods immortal
Quiver, with their figures bent,
In a liquid pediment.

Thence the flood-leat followeth swiftly,
  Where the peasant, spade in hand,
Guideth many a runnel deftly
  Through his fruit and pasture-land;

Oft, the irriguous bank cross-slicing,
Plaited trickles he keeps enticing;
Till their gravelly gush he feels,
Overtaking his brown heels.

27

III

Life—that long hath born the test of
    More than ours could bear, and live—
  Springs anew, to make the best of
    Every chance the Gods may give.

Doum-tree stiffeneth flagging feather ;
Date-leaves cease to cling together ;
Citrons clear their welted rind ;
Vines their mildewed sprays unwind.

Gourds, and melons, spread new lustre
    On their veiny dull shagreen ;
While the starred pomegranates cluster
    Golden balls, with pink between.

IV

Yea, but heaven hath ordered duly,
Lest mankind should wax unruly,
Egypt, garner of all lore,
Narrow as a threshing-floor.

East, and West, lies desolation,
    Infinite, untracked, untold—
Shroud for all of God's creation,
    When the wild blast lifts its fold ;

There eternal melancholy
Maketh all delight unholy ;
As a stricken widow glides
Past a group of laughing brides.

V

Who is this, that so disdaineth
 Dome and desert, fear and fate;
While his jewell'd horse he reineth,
 At Amen-Ra's temple-gate?

He, who crushed the kings of Asia,
Like a pod of colocasia;
Whom the sons of Anak fled,
Puling infants at his tread.

Who, with his own shoulders, lifted
 Thrones of many a conquered land;
Who the rocks of Scythia rifted—
 King Sesostris waves his hand.

VI

Blare of trumpet fills the valley;
Slowly, and majestically,
Swingeth wide, in solemn state,
Lord Amen-Ra's temple-gate.

Thence the warrior-host emergeth,
 Casque, and corselet, spear, and shield;
As the tide of red ore surgeth
 From the furnace-door revealed.

After them, tumultuous rushing,
Mob, and medley, crowd, and crushing;
And the hungry file of priests,
Loosely zoned for larger feasts.

VII

" Look l" The whispered awe enhances
   With a thrill their merry treat;
As one readeth grim romances,
   In a sunny window-seat.

" Look l. It is the maid selected
For the sacrifice expected :
By the Gods, how proud and brave
Steps she to her watery grave l"

Strike up cymbals, gongs, and tabours,
   Clarions, double-flutes, and drums ;
All that bellows, or belabours,
   In a surging discord comes.

VIII

Scarce Duke Iram can keep under
His wild steed's disdain and wonder,
While his large eyes ask alway—
" Dareth man attempt to neigh ?"

He hath snuffed the great Sahara,
   And the mute parade of stars ;
Shall he brook this shrill fanfara,
   Ramshorns, pigskins, screechy jars ?

What hath he to do with rabble ?
Froth is better than their babble ;
Let him toss them flakes of froth,
To pronounce his scorn and wrath.

IX

With his nostrils fierce dilating,
　With his crest a curling sea,
All his volumed power is waiting
　For the will, to set it free.

" Peace, my friend!" The touch he knoweth
　Calms his heart, howe'er it gloweth :
Horse can shame a man, to quell
Passion, where he loveth well.

" Nay, endure we," saith the rider,
　" Till her plighted word be paid ;
Then, though Satan stand beside her,
　God shall help me swing this blade."

X

Lo, upon the deep-piled däis,
Wrought in hallowed looms of Säis,
O'er the impetuous torrent's swoop,
Stands the sacrificial group!

Tall High-priest, with zealot fires
　Blazing in those eyeballs old,
Swathes him, as his rank requires,
　Head to foot, in linen fold.

Seven attendants round him vying,
In a lighter vesture plying,
Four with skirts, and other three
Tunic'd short from waist to knee.

XI

Free among them stands the maiden,
    Clad in white for her long rest;
Crowned with gold, and jewel-laden,
    With a lily on her breast.

Lily is the mark that showeth
Where that pure and sweet heart gloweth;
Here must come, to shed her life,
Point of sacrificial knife.

Here the knife is, cold and gleaming,
    Here the colder butcher band.
Was the true love nought but dreaming,
    Feeble heart, and coward hand?

XII

Strength unto the weak is given,
When their earthly bonds are riven;
Ere the spirit is called away,
Heaven begins its tranquil sway.

Life hath been unstained, and therefore
    Pleasant to look back upon;
But there is not much to care for,
    When the light of love is gone.

Still, though love were twice as fleeting,
Longeth she for one last greeting;
If her eyes might only dwell
Once on his, to say farewell.

XIII

"Glorious Hapi," spake Piromis,
    Lifting high his weapon'd hand ;
"Earth thy footstool, heaven thy dome is,
    We the pebbles on thy strand.

"Thou hast leaped the cubits twenty,
    Dowering us with peace and plenty ;
Mutha shows thee her retreat,
And the desert licks thy feet.

"We have passed through our purgation,
    Once again we are thy kin ;
God, accept our expiation,—
    Maiden pure of mortal sin."

XIV

"Ha!" the king cried, smiling blandly ;
"Ha!" the trumpets answered grandly.
Proudly priest whirled knife on high,
While the maiden bowed—to die.

Sudden, through the ranks beside her,
    Scattering men, like sparks of flint,
Burst a snow-white horse and rider,
    Rapid as the lightning's glint.

One blow hurls Arch-priest to quiver
Headless, in his beloved river,
In the twinkling of an eye,
All the rest are dead, or fly.

XV

Iram, from *Pyropus* sweeping,
  As a mower swathes the rye,
Caught his love, in terror sleeping,
  And her light form swings on high.

"Soul of Khons!" Sesostris shouted,
Striding down the planks blood-grouted—
Into his beard fell something light,
And he spat, and swooned with fright.

What hath made this great king stagger,
  Reel, and shriek—"unclean, unclean!"
Thunderbolt, or flash of dagger?
  Nay, 'twas but a garden bean.

XVI

Brave *Pyropus*, blood-bespattered,
Snorts at men and corpses scattered,
Throws his noble chest more wide,
Leaps into the leaping tide.

Vainly hiss a thousand arrows,
  Launched at random through the foam ;
Every stroke the distance narrows
  Twixt him and his desert home.

Sorely tried, and passion-shaken,
Long amid her foes forsaken,
Now, in tumult of surprise,
Lita knows not where she lies.

34

XVII

Till a bright wave breaks upon her,
  And her clear perceptions wake—
All his valour, prowess, honour,
  Scorn of life, for her poor sake!

Gently then her eyes she raises,
(Eyes, whence all the pure soul gazes)
Softly brings her lips to his—
Lips, wherein the whole heart is.

Let the furious waters welter,
  Let the rough winds roar above;
Waves are warmth, and storms are shelter,
  In the upper heaven of love.

XVIII

Fierce the flood, and wild the danger;
Yet the noble desert-ranger
Flinches not, nor flags, before
He hath brought them safe ashore.

Lives there man, who would have striven,
  Reckless thus of storm and sword,
Leaped into the gulf, and given
  Heart and soul, to please his Lord?

With caresses they have plied him,
Hand in hand they kneel beside him,
While their mutual vows they plight
To the God of life and light.

XIX

Ha! What meaneth yon sword-flashing?
  Trumps, and shouts from wave and isle?
Lô, the warrior galleys dashing,
  To avenge insulted Nile!

Haste! The brave steed, leaping lightly,
'Neath his double burden sprightly,
Challenges, with scornful note,
Every horse in Pharaoh's boat.

King of Egypt, curb thy rages;
  Lo, how trouble should be borne!
Memnon soothes the woe of ages,
  With a sweet song, every morn.

KADISHA; OR, THE FIRST JEALOUSY
AN EASTERN LEGEND

HERE IS A CURIOUS LEGEND AS TO THE ORIGIN OF JEALOUSY. WHEN ADAM AND EVE WERE IN PARADISE, THE FORMER WAS ACCUSTOMED TO RETIRE AT EVENTIDE TO THE RECESSES OF THE GARDEN, FOR THE PURPOSE OF PRAYER. ON ONE OF THESE OCCASIONS THE DEVIL APPEARED TO EVE, AND INFORMED HER THAT HER SOLITUDE WAS TO BE ACCOUNTED FOR BY THE ATTRACTIONS OF ANOTHER FAIR ONE. EVE REPLIED THAT IT COULD NOT BE SO, AS SHE WAS THE ONLY WOMAN IN EXISTENCE. "IF I SHOW YOU ANOTHER, WILL YOU BELIEVE ME?" RETURNED THE EVIL ONE, AND PRODUCED A MIRROR, IN WHICH SHE SAW HER OWN REFLECTION, AND MISTOOK IT FOR

The citron, stephanote, and rose,
  Pomegranate, hoya, calycanth,
  And yet unwanted amaranth,
Were sweetness in repose:

II

When rivulets were loth to creep,
  Except unto the pillow moss,
And distant lake, encurtained deep,
  Was but a silver thread across
    The eyes of sleep:

When nightingales, in the sycamore,
  Sang low and soft, as an echo dreaming;
And slept the moon upon heaven's shore—
  The tidal shore of heaven, beaming
    With lazuled ore:

When new-born earth was fain to lean
  In Summer's arms, recovering
  The unaccustomed toil of Spring,
Why slept not Eve, their Queen?

III

Upon a smooth fern-mantled stone
  She sat, and watched the wicket-gate,
Not timid in her woman's throne,
  Nor lonely in her sinless state,
    Though all alone;

43

For having spread her simple board
  With grapes, and peaches, milk, and flowers,
She strewed sweet mastic o'er the sward,
  And waited through the bridal hours
    Step of her lord.

Such innocence around her breathed,
  And freshness of young nature's play,
  The sensitive plant shrank not away,
And cactus' swords were sheathed.

IV

The vision of her beauty fell,
  Like music on a moonlit place,
Or trembles of a silver bell,
  Or memories of a sacred face,
    Too dear to tell:

The grace that wandered free of laws,
  The look that lit the heart's confession,
Had never dreamed how fair it was;
  Nor guessed that purity's expression
    Is beauty's cause:

No more that unenquiring heart
  Perused the sweet home of her breast,
  Than turtle-doves unline their nest
To scan the outer part.

V

Although, in all that garden fair,
   Whate'er delight abode, or grew,
Flowers, and trees, and balmy air,
   Fountains, and birds, and heaven blue
     Beyond compare :

In her their various charms had met,
   And grown more varied by combining,
As budded plants do give and get,
   Each inmate doubling while resigning
     His several debt :

And yet she nursed one joy, above
   Her thousand charms, nor born of them,
   But blooming on a single stem—
Her true faith in her love.

VI

And though, before she heard his foot,
   The moon had climbed the homestead palm,
Flinging to her the shadowed fruit,
   And tree-frogs ceased to break the calm,
     And birds were mute,

With sudden transport ever new,
   She blushed, and sprang from forth the bower,
Her eyes as bright as moon-lit dew,
   Her bosom glad as snow-veiled flower,
     When sun shines through ;

He, with a natural dignity
Untaught self-consciousness by harm,
Sustained her with his manly arm,
And smiled upon her glee.

VII

Next day, when early evening shone
Along the walks of Paradise,
Strewing with gold the hills, her throne,
Embarrassing the winds with spice
(Too rich a loan),

Fair Eve was in her bower of ease,
A cool arcade of fruit and flowers,
From North and East enclasped by trees,
But open to the Western showers,
And Southern breeze.

Here followed she her gardening trade,
Her favourites' simple needs attending,
And singing soft, above them bending,
A song herself had made.

VIII

In evening's calm, she walked between
The tints and shades of rich delight,
While overhead came, arching green,
Many a shrub and parasite,
To crown their Queen ;

There laughed the joy of the rose, among
  Myrtle and Iris, heaven's eye,
Magnole, with cups of moonlight hung,
  And Fuchsia's sunny chandlery,
    And coral tongue;

And where the shy brook fluttered through,
  Nepenthe held her chalice leaf
  (Undrained as yet by human grief),
And broad Nymphæa grew.

IX

But where the path bent towards the wood,
  Across it hung a sombre screen,
The deadly night-shade, leaden-hued;
  And there behind it, darkly seen,
    A Being stood:

The form, if any form it had,
  Was likest to a nightly vision
In mantle of amazement clad,
  A terror-sense, without precision,
    Of something bad.

A tremble chilled the forest shade,
  A roving lion turned and fled,
  The birds cowered home in hush of dread;
But Eve was not afraid.

X

She stood before him, sweetly bold,
 To keep him from her garden shrine,
With hair that fell, a shower of gold,
 Around her figure's snowy line
  And rosy mould :

He (with a re-awakened sense
 Of goodness, long for ever lost,
And angel beauty's pure defence)
 Shrank back, unable to accost
  Such innocence :

But envy soon scoffed down his shame ;
 And with a smile, designed for fawning,
 But like hell's daybreak sickly dawning,
His crafty accents came.

XI

" Sweet ignorance, 'tis sad and hard
 To break thy fond confiding spell ;
And my soft heart hath such regard
 For thine, that I will never tell
  What may be spared."

He turned aside, o'erwhelmed with pain,
 And drew a sigh of deep compassion :
She trembled, flushed, and gazed again,
 And prayed him quick, in woman's fashion,
  To speak it plain :

48

" Then, if thou must be taught to grieve,
    And scorn the guile thou hast adored—
The man who calls himself thy lord,
Where goes he, every eve?"

XII

" Nay, then," she cried, " if that be all,
    I care not what thou hast to say;
The guile that lurks therein is small—
    My husband but retires to pray,
        At evening call."

" To pray? Oh yes, and on his knees
    May-hap to find a lovely being:
Devotions so devout as these
    Are best at night, with no one seeing,
        Among the trees."

She blushed as deep as modesty,
    Then glancing back as bright as pride,
" What woman can he find," she cried,
" In all the world, but me?"

XIII

He laughed with a superior sneer,
    Enough to shake e'en woman's faith;
" Wilt thou believe me, simple dear,
    If I am able now," he saith,
        " To show her here?"

She cried aloud with gladsome heart,
  " Be that the test whereon to try thee;
Nature and heaven shall take my part:
  Come, show this rival; I defy thee
    And all thy art."

A mirror, held in readiness,
  He set upright before her feet—
" Now can thy simple charms compete
With beauty such as this?"

XIV

A lovelier sight therein she saw
  Than ever yet had charmed her eyes,
A fairer picture, void of flaw,
  Than any, even Paradise
    Itself, could draw;

A woman's form of perfect grace,
  In shadowy softness delicate;
Though flushed by sunset's rich embrace,
  A white rose could not imitate
    Her innocent face:

Then, through the deepening glance of fear,
  The shaft of doubt came quivering,
  The sorrow-shaft—a sigh its wing,
And for its barb a tear.

50

XV

" Ah me!" she cried, " too true it is !
    A simple homely thing, like Eve,
Hath not a chance to rival this,
    But must resign herself to grieve
        O'er by-gone bliss.

" Till now it was enough for me
    To be what God our Father made ;
Oh, Adam, I was proud to be
    (As I have felt, and thou hast said)
        A part of thee.

" No marvel that my lord can spare
    His true and heaven-appointed bride.
And yet affection might have tried
    To fancy me as fair."

XVI

The Tempter, glorying in his wile,
    Hath ta'en his mirror and withdrawn ;
Again the flowers look up and smile,
    And brightens off from air and lawn
        The taint of guile.

But smiles come not again to Eve,
    Nor brightens off her dark reflection :
Her garland-crown she hath ceased to weave,
    And, plucking, maketh no selection ;
        Only to grieve.

She feels a dewy radiance steep
　The languid petals of her eyes,
　And hath another sad surprise,
To know the way to weep.

PART II

THE tears were still in woman's eyes,
When morn awoke on Paradise ;
And still her sense of shame forbade
To tell her grievance, or upbraid ;
Nor knew she which was dearer cost,
To seek him, or to shun him most.
Then Adam, willing to believe
 A heart by casual fancy moved
 Would soon come back, at voice she loved,
Addressed his song to Eve.

I

" COME fairest, while the morn is fair,
 And dews are bright as yon clear eyes ;
 Calm down this tide of troubled hair,
Forget with me all other sighs
 Than summer air.

" Like me, the woodland shadows roam
 At light (their fairer comrade's) side ;
And peace and joy salute our home ;
 And lo, the sun in all his pride—
 My sunshine, come !

" The fawns and birds, that know our call,
 Are waiting for our presence—see,
 They wait my presence, love ; and thee,
The most desired of all.

II

"The trees, which thought it grievous thing
　To weep their own sweet leaves away,
Untaught as yet how soon the Spring
Upon their nestled heads should lay
　Her callow wing—

"The trees, whereat we smiled again,
　To see them, in their growing wonder,
Suppose their buds were verdant rain,
Until the gay winds rustled under
　Their feathered train,

"Lo, now they stand in braver mien,
　And, claiming stronger shadow-right,
　Make prisoner of the intrusive light,
And strew the winds with green.

III

"Of all the flowers that bow the head,
　Or gaze erect on sun and sky,
Not one there is, declines to shed,
Or standeth up, to qualify
　His incense-meed :

"Of all that blossom one by one,
　Or join their lips in loving cluster,
Not one hath now resolved alone,
Or taken counsel, that his lustre
　Shall be unshown.

54

"So let thy soul a blossom be,
    To breathe the fragrance of its praise,
    And lift itself, in early days,
To Him who fosters thee.

IV

"Of all the founts, bedropped with light,
    Or silver-tress d with shade of trees,
Not one there is, but sprinkles bright
    It's plume of freshness on the breeze,
    And jewelled flight:

"Of all that hush among the moss,
    Or babble to the lily-vases,
Not one there is but purls across
    A gush of the delight, that causes
    It's limpid gloss.

"So let thy heart a fountain be,
    To rise in sparkling joy, and fall
    In dimpled melody—and all
For love of home, and me."

V

The only fount her heart became
    Rose quick with sighs, and fell in tears;
While pink upon her white cheek came,
    (Like apple-blossom among pear's)
    The tinge of shame.

55

Her husband, pierced with new alarm,
  Bent nigh to ask of her distresses,
Enclasping her with sheltering arm,
  Unwinding by discreet caresses,
    The thread of harm.

Then she, with sobs of slow relief
  (For silence is the jail of care)
  Confessed, for him to heal or share,
The first of human grief.

VI

" I cannot look on thee, and think
  That thou has ceased to hold me dear;
I cannot break the loosened link:
  When thou, my only one, art near,
    How can I shrink?

" So it were better, love—I mean,
  My lord, it is more wise and right—
That I, as one whose day hath been,
  Should keep my pain from pleasure's sight,
    And dwell unseen.

" And—though it break my heart to say—
  However sad my loneliness,
  I fear thou wouldst rejoice in this—
To have me far away.

VII

" I know not how it is with man,
    Perhaps his nature is to change,
On finding consort fairer than—
    But oh, I cannot so arrange
      My nature's plan !

" And haply thou hast never thought
    To vex, or make me feel forsaken ;
But, since to thee the thing was nought,
    Supposed 'twould be as gaily taken,
      As lightly brought.

" Yet, is it strange that I repine,
    And feel abased in lonely woe,
    To lose thy love—or e'en to know
That half of it is mine ?

VIII

" For whom have I on earth but thee,
    What heart to love, or home to bless ?
Albeit I was wrong, I see,
    To think my husband took no less
      Delight in me.

" But even now, if thou wilt stay,
    Or try at least no more to wander,
And let me love thee, day by day,
    Till time, or habit, make thee fonder
      (If so it may)—

i

"Thou shalt have one more truly bent,
  In homely wise, on serving thee,
  Than any stranger e'er can be;
And Eve shall seem content."

IX

Not loud she wept—but hope could hear;
  Sweet hope, who in his lifelong race
Made terms, to win the goal from fear,
  That each alternate step should trace
    A smile and tear.

But Adam, lost in wide amaze,
  Regarded her with troubled glances,
Misdoubting 'neath her steady gaze,
  Himself to be in strange romances,
    And dreamy haze:

Then questioning in hurried voice,
  And scarcely waiting her replies,
  He spoke, and showed the true surprise
That made her soul rejoice.

X

She told him what the Tempter said,
  And what her frightened self had seen,
(That form in loveliness arrayed,
  With modest face, and graceful mien)
    And how displayed.
58

Then well-content to show his bride
　　The worldly knowledge he possessed,
(That world whereof was none beside)
　　He laid his hand upon his breast,
　　　　And thus replied :—

" Wife, mirror'd here too deep to see,
　" A little way down yonder path,
　:" And I will show the form which hath
" Enchanted thee, and me."

XI

Kadisha is a streamlet fair,
　　Which hurries down the pebbled way,
As one who hath small time to spare,
　　So far to go, so much to say
　　　　To summer air ;

Sometimes the wavelets wimple in
　　O'erlapping tiers of crystal shelves,
And little circles dimple in,
　　As if the waters quaffed themselves,
　　　　The while they spin :

Thence in a clear pool, overbent
　　With lotus-tree and tamarind flower,
　　Empearled, and lulled in golden bower,
Kadisha sleeps content.

And, bending o'er in sweet surprise,
  Perused, with simple child's delight,
  The flowing hair, and forehead white,
And soft inquiring eyes.

XIV

Then, blushing to a fairer tint
  Than waves might ever hope to catch,
" I see," she cried, " a lovely print ;
  But surely I can never match
  This lily glint !

" So pure, so innocent, and bright,
  So charming free, without endeavour,
So fancy-touched with pensive light !
  I think that I could gaze for ever,
  With new delight.

" And now that rose-bud in my hair,
  Perhaps it should be placed above—
  And yet, I will not change it, love,
Since thou hast set it there.

XV

" Vain Eve, why glory thus in Eve?
  What matter for thy form or face ?
Thy beauty is, if love believe
  Thee worthy of that treasured place
  Thou ne'er shalt leave.

63

MOUNT ARAFA
IN TWO PARTS

"Mount Arafa, situated about a mile from Mecca, is held in great veneration by the Mussulmans, as a place very proper for penitence. Its fitness in this respect is accounted for by a tradition that Adam and Eve, on being banished out of Paradise, in order to do penance for their transgression were parted from each other, and after a separation of six score years, met again upon this mountain."

OCKLEY'S "HISTORY OF THE SARACENS," p. 60.

THE PARTING

I

RIVEN away from Eden's
   gate
(With blazing falchions
   fenced about)
Into a desert desolate,
  A miserable pair came out,
   To meet their fate.

To wander in a world of woe,
  To ache and starve, to burn and shiver,
With every living thing their foe—
  The fire of God above, the river
   Of death below.

Of home, of hope, of Heaven bereft;
  It is the destiny of man

To cower beneath his Maker's ban,
And hide from his own theft !

II

The father of a world unborn—
Who hath begotten death, ere life—
In sullen silence plods forlorn ;
His love and pride in his fair wife
Are rage and scorn.

Instead of Angel ministers,
What hath he now but fiends devouring
Instead of grapes and melons, burs ;
In lieu of manna, crab and souring—
By whose fault ? Hers !

Alack, good sire of feeble knees,
New penance waits thee ; since—when thus
Thou shouldst have wept for all of us—
Thou mournest thine own ease !

III

The mother of all loving wives
(Condemned unborn to many a tear)
Is fain to take his hand, and strives
In sorrow to be doubly dear—
But shame deprives.

68

The shame, the woe, the black surprise,
   That love's first dream should have such ending,
To weep, and wipe neglected eyes!
   Oh loss of true love, far transcending
      Lost Paradise!

For is it faith, that cannot live
   One gloomy hour, and soar above
The clouds of fate?   And is it love,
   That will not e'en forgive?

IV

The houseless monarch of the earth
   Hath quickly found what empire means;
For while he scoffs with bitter mirth,
   And curses, after Eden's scenes,
      This dreary dearth.

A snake, that twined in playful zeal,
   But yester morn, around his ankle,
Now driven along the dust to steal,
   Steals up, and leaves its venom'd rankle
      Deep in his heel.

He groans awhile.   He seeks anon
   For comfort to this first of pain,
   Where all his sons to-day are fain;
He seeks—but Eve is gone!

PART I—ADAM

O'er hill, and highland, moor, and plain,
A hundred years, he seeks in vain;
O'er hill and plain, a hundred years,
He pours the sorrow no one hears;
Yet finds, as wildest mourners find,
Some ease of heart in toil of mind.

I

" YE mountains, that forbid the day,
Ye glens, that are the steps of night,
How long amid you must I stray,
Deserted, banished from God's sight,
And cast away?

" Ye trees and flowers the Lord hath made,
Ye beasts, to my good-will committed—
Although your trust hath been betrayed—
Not long ago ye would have pitied
Your old comrade.

" Oh, nature, noblest when alone,
Albeit I love your outward part;
The nature that enthrals my heart
Must be more like my own.

72

II

" The Maker once appointed me—
　I know not, and I care not why—
The lord of everything I see,
　Or if they walk, or swim, or fly,
　　Whate'er they be.

" And all the earth whereon they dwell,
　And all the heavens they are inhaling,
And powers, whereof I cannot tell—
　Dark miscreants, supine and wailing,
　　Until I fell.

" 'Twas good and glorious to believe;
　But now my majesty is o'er;
And I would give it all, and more,
For one sweet glimpse of Eve.

III

" For what is glory, what is power?
　And what the pride of standing first?
A twig struck down by a thunder shower,
　A crown of thistle to quench the thirst,
　　A sun-scorched flower.

" God grant the men who spring from me,
　As knowledge waxeth deep and splendid,
To find a loftier pedigree
　Than any by the Lord intended—
　　Frog, slug, or tree!

73

"So shall they live, without the grief
Of having womankind to love,
Find nought below, and less above,
And be their own belief.

IV

"So weak was I, so poorly taught,
By any but my Maker's voice,
Too happy to indulge in thought,
Which gives me little to rejoice,
And ends in nought.

"But now and then, my path grows clear,
My mind casts off its grim confusion,
When I have chanced on goodly cheer:
Then happiness seems no delusion,
Even down here.

"With love and faith, to bless the curse,
To heal the mind by touch of heart,
To make me feel my better part,
And fight against the worse.

V

"It may be that I did o'erprize,
Above the Giver, that rare gift,
Ungird my will for softer ties,
And hold my manhood little thrift
To woman's eyes.

74

" So fair she was, so full of grace,
    So innocent with coy caresses,
  So proud to step at my own pace;
    So rosy through her golden tresses;.
      And such a face !

" Suffice my sins ; I'll ne'er approve
    A thought against my faithful Eve ;.
    Suffice my sins.; I'll never believe
  That it was one to love.

VI

" Oh, love, if e'er this desert plain,,
    Where I must sweat with axe and spade,
  Shall hold a people sprung from twain,
    Or better made by Him, who made
      That pair in vain..

" Shall any know, as we have known,
    Thy rapture, terror, vaunting, fretting,
  Profound despair, ecstatic tone;
    Crowning of reason, and upsetting
      Of reason's throne?

" Bright honey quaff'd from cells of gall,
    Or crimson sting from creamy rose—
    Thy heavenly half from Eden flows,
  Thy venom from our fall."

Awhile he ceased; for scorching woe
Had made a drought of vocal flow;
When hungry, weary, desolate,
A fox crept home to his den's gate.
The sight brought Adam's memory back,
And touched him with a keener lack.

VII

" Home! Where is home? Of old I thought
   (Or felt in mystery of bliss)
That so divinely was I wrought
   As not to care for that or this,
     And value nought;

" But sit or saunter, rest or roam,
   Regarding all things most sublimely,
As if enthroned on heaven's dome;
   Away with paltry and untimely
     Hankerings for *Home!*

" But now the weary heart is fain
   For shelter in some lowly nest—
To sink upon a softer breast,
   And smile away its pain.

VIII

" For me, what home, what hope is left?
   What difference of good or ill?
Of all I ever loved bereft,
   Disgraced, discarded, outlawed still,
     For one small theft!

"I sicken of my skill and pride;
  I work, without a bit of caring.
The world is waste, the world is wide;
  Why make good things, with no one sharing
    Them at my side?

"What matters how I dwell, or die?
  Away with such a niggard life!
  The Lord hath robbed me of my wife;
And life is only I.

IX

"God, who hast said it is not good
  For man, thy son, to live alone;
Is everlasting solitude,
  When once united bliss was known,
    A livelier food?

"Can'st thou suppose it right or just,
  When thine own creature so misled us,
In virtue of our simple trust,
  To torture us like this, and tread us
    Back into dust?

"Oh, fool I am. Oh, rebel worm!
  If, when immortal, I was slain,
  For daring to impugn his reign,
How shall I, thus infirm?

77

X

" Woe me, poor me ! No humbler yet,
   For all the penance on me laid !
Forgive me, Lord, if I forget
   That I am but what Thou hast made,
      My soul Thy debt !

" Inspire me to survey the skies,
   And tremble at their golden wonder,
To learn the space that *I* comprise,
   At once to marvel, and to ponder,
      And drop mine eyes.

" And grant me—for I do but find,
   In seeking more than God hath shown,
   I scorn His power and lose my own—
Grant me a lowly mind.

XI

" A lowly mind ! Thou wondrous sprite,
   Whose frolics make their master weep ;
Anon, endowed with eagle's flight,
   Anon, too impotent to creep,
      Or blink aright ;—

" Howe'er, thy trumpery flashes play
   Among the miracles above thee,
Be taught to feel thy Maker's sway,
   To labour, so that He shall love thee,
      And guide thy way.

78

" Be led, from out the cloudy dreams
    Of thy too visionary part,
    To listen to the whispering heart,
    And curb thine own extremes.

XII

" Then hope shall shine from heaven, and give
    To fruit of hard work, sunny cheek,
    And flowers of grace and love revive,
    And shrivelled pasturage grow sleek,
    And corn shall thrive.

" Beholding gladness, Eve and I,
    Enfolding it also in each other,
    May talk of heaven without a sigh ;
    Because our heaven in one another
    Love shall supply.

" For courage, faith, and bended knees,
    By stress of patience, cure distress,
    And turn wild *Love-in-idleness*
    Into the true *Heartsease.*"

The Lord breathed on the first of men,
And strung his limbs to strength again ;
He scorned a century of ill,
And girt his loins to climb the parting hill.

79

PART II—EVE

Meanwhile through lowland, holt, and glade,
Sad Eve her lonely travel made ;
Not fierce, or proud, but well content
To own the righteous punishment ;
Yet found, as gentle mourners find,
The heart's confession soothe the mind.

I

" Y E valleys, and ye waters vast,
    Who answer all that look on you
    With shadows of themselves, that last
As long as they, and are as true—
    Where hath he past?

" Oh woods, and heights of rugged stone,
    Oh weariness of sky above me,
For ever must I pine and moan,
    With none to comfort, none to love me,
        Alone, alone?

" Thou bird, that hoverest at heaven's gate,
    Or cleavest limpid lines of air,
    Return—for thou hast one to care—
Return to thy dear mate.
        80

II

" For me, no joy of earth or sky,
 No commune with the things I see,
But dreary converse of the eye
 With worlds too grand to look at me—
  No smile, no sigh !

" In vain I fall upon my knees,
 In vain I weep and sob for ever ;
All other miseries have ease,
 All other prayers have ruth—but never
  Any for these.

" Are we endowed with heavenly breath,
 And God's own form, that we should win
 A proud priority of sin,
And teach creation death ?

III

" Nay, that is too profound for me,
 Too lofty for a fallen thing.
More keenly do I feel than see ;
 Far liefer would I, than take wing,
  Beneath it be.

" The night—the dark—will soon be here,
 The gloom that doth my heart appal so !
How can I tell what may be near ?
 My faith is in the Lord—but also
  He hath made fear.

" I quail, I cower, I strive to flee ;
Though oft I watched without affright,
The stern magnificence of night,
When Adam was with me

IV

" My husband ! Ah, I thought sometime
That I could do without him well,
Communing with the heaven at prime,
And in my womanhood could dwell
Calm and sublime.

" Declining, with a playful strife,
All thoughts below my own transcendence,
All common-sense of earth and life,
And counting it a poor dependence
To be his wife.

" But now I know, by trouble's test,
How little my poor strength can bear,
What folly wisdom is, whene'er
The grief is in the breast !

V

" The grief is in my breast, because
I have not always been as kind
As woman should, by nature's laws,
But showed sometimes a wilful mind,
Carping at straws.

"While he, perhaps, with larger eyne,
  Was pleased, instead of vexed, at seeing
Some little petulance in mine,
  And loved me all the more, for being
    Not too divine.

"Until the pride became a snare,
  The reason a deceit, wherein
I dallied face to face with sin,
  And made a mortal pair.

VI.

"Dark sin, the deadly foe of love,
  All bowers of bliss thou shalt infest,
Implanting thorns the flowers above,
  And one black feather in the breast
    Of purest dove.

"Almighty Father, once our friend,
  And ready even now to love us,
Thy pitying gaze upon us bend,
  And through the tempest-clouds above us
    Thine arm extend.

"That so thy children may begin
  In lieu of bliss, to earn content,
  And find that sinful Eve was meant
Not only for a sin."

Awhile she ceased; for memory's flow
Had drowned the utterance of woe;
Until a young hind crossed the lawn,
And fondly trotted forth her fawn,
Whose frolics of delight made Eve,
As in a weeping vision, grieve.

VII

" For me, poor me, no hope to learn
    That sweeter bliss than Paradise,
The joy that makes a mother yearn
    O'er that bright message from the skies
    Her pains do earn.

" She stoops entranced ; she fears to stir,
    Or think ; lest e'en a thought endanger
(While two enraptured hearts confer)
    That wonderful and wondering stranger,
    Come home to her.

" He watches her, in solemn style ;
    A world of love flows to and fro ;
    He smiles ; that he may learn to know
His mother by her smile.

VIII

" Oh, bliss, that to all other bliss
    Shall be as sunrise unto night,
Or heaven to such a place as this,
    Or God's own voice, with angels bright,
    To serpent's hiss !

" Have I betrayed thee, or cast by
    The pledge in which my soul delighted—
That all this wrong and misery
    Should be avenged at last, and righted,
        And so should I ?

" Belike, they look on me as dead,
    Those fiends that found me soft and sweet;
    But God hath promised me one treat—
To crush that serpent's head !

IX

" Revenge ! Oh, heaven, let some one rise,
    Some woman, since revenge is small,—
Who shall not care about its size,
    If only she can get it all,
        For those black lies !

" Poor Adam is too good and great,
    I felt it, though he said so little—
To hate his foes, as I can hate—
    And pay them every jot, and tittle,
        At their own rate.

" For was there none but I to blame ?
    God knows that if, instead of me,
    There had been any other she,
She would have done the same.

X

" Poor me! Of course the whole disgrace,
  In spite of reason, falls on me :
And so all women of my race,
  In pure right, shall be reason-free,
    In every case.

" It shall not be in power of man
  To bind them to their own contentions ;
But each shall speak, as speak she can,
  And start anew with fresh inventions,
    Where she began.

" And so shall they be dearer still ;
  For man shall ne'er suspect in them
  The plucking of the fatal stem,
That brought him all his ill.

XI

" And when hereafter—as there must,
  Since He, that made us, so hath sworn—
From that whereof we are, the dust,
  And whereunto we shall return
    In higher trust—

" There spring a grand and countless race,
  Replenishing this vast possession,
Till life hath won a larger space
  Than death, by quick and fair succession
    Of health and grace ;

"They too shall find as I have found
    The grief, that lifts its head on high,
    A dewy bud the sun shall dry—
But not while on the ground.

XII

"Then men shall love their wives again,
    Allowing for the frailer kind,
Content to keep the heart's Amen,
    Content to own the turns of mind
        Beyond their ken.

"And wives shall in their lords be blest,
    Their higher sense of right perceiving
(When possible) with love their test;
    Exalting, solacing, believing
        All for the best.

"And for the best shall all things be,
    If God once more will shine around,
    And lift my husband from the ground,
And teach him to lift me."

New faith inspired the first of wives,
She smiles, and drooping hope revives;
She scorns a hundred years of woe,
And binds her hair, because the breezes blow.

87

THE MEETING

I

THE wind is hushed, the moon is bright,
   More stars on heaven than may be told ;
   Young flowers are coying with the light,
That softly tempts them to unfold,
   And trust the night.

What form comes bounding from above
   Down Arafa, the mountain lonely,
Afraid to scare its long-lost dove,
   Yet swift as joy—" It can be only,
      Only my love!"

What shape is that—too fair to leave
   On Arafa, the mountain lone ?
   So trembling, and so faint—" My own,
It must be my own Eve!"

II

As when the mantled heavens display
   The glory of the morning glow,
And spread the mountain heights with day,
   And bid the clouds and shadows go
      Trooping away,

The Spirit of the Lord arose,
   And made the earth and heaven to quiver,
And scattered all his hellish foes,
   And deigned his good stock to deliver
      From all their woes.

So long the twain had strayed apart,
   That each as at a marvel gazed,
   With eyes abashed, and brain amazed ;
While heart enquired of heart.

III

Our God hath made a fairer thing
   Than fairest dawn of summer day—
A gentle, timid, fluttering,
   Confessing glance, that seeks alway
     Rest for its wing.

A sweeter sight than azure skies,
   Or golden star thereon that glideth ;
And blest are they who see it rise,
   For, if it cometh, it abideth
     In woman's eyes.

   The first of men such blessing sued ;
    The first of women smiled consent ;
    For husband, wife and home it meant,
And no more solitude!

IV

We trample now the faith of old,
   We make our Gods of dream and doubt ;
Yet life is but a tale untold,
   Without one heart to love, without
     One hand to hold—

THE WELL OF SAINT JOHN

The old well of Saint John, in the parish of Newton-Nottage, Glamorganshire, has a tide of its own, which appears to run exactly counter to that of the sea, some half-mile away. The water is beautifully bright and fresh, and the quaint dome among the lonely sands is regarded with some awe and reverence.

He

"THERE is plenty of room for two in here,
Within the steep tunnel of old grey stone;
And the well is so dark, and the spring so clear,
It is quite unsafe to go down alone."

She

"It is perfectly safe, depend upon it,
For a girl who can count the steps, like me;
And if ever I saw dear mother's bonnet,
It is there on the hill by the old ash-tree."

He

" There is nobody but Rees Hopkin's cow
    Watching the dusk on the milk-white sea ;
'Tis the time and the place for a life-long vow,
    Such as I owe you, and you owe me."

She

" Oh, Willie, how can I, in this dark well ?
    I shall drop the brown pitcher if you let go ;
The long roof is murmuring like a sea-shell,
    And the shadows are shuddering to and fro."

He

" 'Tis the sound of the ebb, in Newton Bay,
    Quickens the spring, as the tide grows less ;
Even as true love flows alway
    Counter the flood of the world's success."

She

" There is no other way for love to flow,
    Whenever it springs in a woman's breast ;
With the tide of its own heart it must go,
    And run contráry to all the rest."

He

" Then fill the sweet cup of your hand, my love,
    And pledge me your maiden faith thereon,
By the touch of the letter'd stone above,
    And the holy water of Saint John."

94

She

"Oh, what shall I say?   My heart sinks low;
　My fingers are cold, and my hand too flat,
Is love to be measured by handfuls so;
　And you know that I love you—without that."

　　　*　　　*　　　*　　　*

They stooped, in the gleam of the faint light, over
　The print of themselves on the limpid gloom;
And she lifted her full palm toward her lover,
　With her lips preparing the words of doom.

But the warm heart rose, and the cold hand fell,
　And the pledge of her faith sprang sweet and clear,
From a holier source than the old Saint's well,
　From the depth of a woman's love—a tear.

PAUSIAS AND GLYCERA; OR, THE FIRST FLOWER-PAINTER
A STORY IN THREE SCENES

(Plin. Nat. Hist., xxxv. 11)

SCENE I:—*Outside the gate of Sicyon—Morning. Glycera weaving garlands, Pausias stands admiring.*

Pausias

E Gods, I thought myself the Prince of Art,
By Phœbus, and the Muses set apart,
To smite the critic with his own complaint,
And teach the world the proper way to paint.
But lo, a young maid trips out of a wood,
And what becomes of all I understood?

96

I stand and stare; I could not draw a line,
If ninety Muses came, instead of nine.
Thy name, fair maiden, is a debt to me;
Teach him to speak, whom thou hast taught to see.
Myself already some repute have won,
For I am Pausias, Brietes' son.
To boast behoves me not, nor do I need,
But often wish my friends to win the meed.
So shall they now; no more will I pursue
    The beaten track, but try what thou hast shown,
    New forms, new curves, new harmonies of tone,
New dreams of heaven, and how to make them true."

Glycera

"Fair Sir, 'tis only what I plucked this morn,
Kind nature's gift, ere you and I were born.
Through mossy woods, and watered vales, I roam,
While day is young, and bring my treasure home;
Each lovely bell so tenderly I bear,
It knoweth not my fingers from the air.
Lo now, they scarce acknowledge their surprise,
And how the dewdrops sparkle in their eyes!"

Pausias

"Because the sun shines out of thine. But hush,
To praise a face praiseworthy, makes it blush.
I am not of the youths who find delight,
In every pretty thing that meets their sight.
My father is the sage of Sicyon;
And I—well, he is proud of such a son."

97   O

Glycera

" And proud am I, my mother's child to be,
And earn for her the life she gave to me.
Her name is Myrto of the silver hair,
Not famed for wisdom, but loved everywhere."

Pausias

" Then whence thine art ?   Hath Phœbus given thee boon
Of wreath and posy, fillet and festoon ?
Of tint and grouping, balance, depth, and tone—
Lo, I could cast my palette down, and groan ! "

Glycera

" No art, fair sir, hath ever crossed my thought,
The lesson I delight in comes untaught.
The flowers around me take their own sweet way,
They tell me what they wish—and I obey.
Unlike poor us, they feel no spleen or spite,
But earn their joy, by ministering delight.
So loved and cherished, each may well suppose
Itself at home again just where it grows.
No dread have they of what the Fates may bring,
But trust their Gods, and breathe perpetual Spring."

Pausias

" Fair child of Myrto, simple-hearted maid,
Thy innocence doth arrogance upbraid.
Ye Gods, I pray you make a flower of me ;
That I may dwell with nature, and with thee."

Glycera
" I see the brave sun leap the city wall !
The gates swing wide ; I hear the herald's call.
The Archon hath proclaimed the market-day ;
And mother will shed tears at my delay.
The priest of Zeus hath ordered garlands three ;
And while I tarry, who will wait for me ? "

Pausias
" No picture have I sold for many a moon,
But fortune must improve her habits soon ;
Then will I purchase all thy stock-in-trade,
    And thou shalt lead me to thy bower of green,
    There will I paint the flowers, and thee their Queen—
The Queen of flowers, that nevermore shall fade."

Glycera
" I know a wood-nymph, who her dwelling hath
Among the leaves, and far beyond the path,
With myrtle and with jasmin roofed across,
Enlaced with vine, and carpeted with moss,
Whose only threshold is a plaited brook,
Whereby the primrose at herself may look ;
While birds of song melodious make the air—
But oh ! I must not take a stranger there."

Pausias
" Nay, but a friend. No stranger now am I.
Good art is pledge of perfect modesty.
From chastened heights the painter glanceth down ;
No maid can fear a youth who loves renown."

99

Glycera
" Thy words are trim. If mother deems them true,
Thou shalt come with me.   But till then, adieu ! "
[Exit.
Pausias
" O ! where am I ?   The mind is all for art—
But one warm breath transforms it into heart."

SCENE II :—*A Wood near Sicyon.   Pausias with his
easel, &c.   Glycera carrying flowers.*

Pausias
" Confounded tangle ! Who could paint all this ?
A bear might hug him, or a serpent hiss !
For love of nature justly am I famed ;
But when she goes so far as this, she ought to be ashamed."

Glycera
" Nay, be not frightened by a small affray,
Pure love of nature cannot pave its way.
But lo, where yonder coney-tracks begin,
My nymph hath made her favourite bower within.
Yon oak hath reared its rugged antlers thus,
Before Deucalion lived, or Dædalus.
Inside her woodland Majesty doth keep
A world of wonders—if one dared to peep—
Of things that burrow, glide, spin webs, or creep ;
Strange creatures, which before they live must die,
And plants that hunt for prey, and flowers that fly ! "

Pausias
" My love of nature freezes in a trice ;
  I loathe all earwigs, beetles, and wood-lice.
  Outside her bower the lady must remain,
  If she doth wish to have her portrait ta'en."

Glycera
" 'Tis not the lady thou must paint—but me."

Pausias
" Aha, that will I, with a glow of glee.
  But when I offered, somebody was vexed,
  And blushed, and frowned, and longed to say, 'what next?'"

Glycera
" A painter's tongue hath learnt to paint, I trow.
  But oh that order—I remember now—
  For twenty chaplets, from the priest of Zeus !
  Ah, what a grand majestic Hiereus ! "
  So pleased he was that morning with those three,
  And such a customer he means to be !

Pausias
" The priest of *Dis* ! a scoundrel with three wives !
  I'll pull his triple beard, if he arrives."

Glycera
" High words and threats profane this hallowed place,
  Where Time rebukes the fuss of human race.
  And gentle sir, what harm hath he done thee ?
  It is my mother whom he comes to see.

Lo, how the Gods our puny wrath deride,
With peace and beauty spread on every side !
This earth with pleasure of the Spring complete,
Too bright to dwell on, were it not so sweet.
No theft of man it's affluence impairs,
A thousand flowers, without a loss, it spares ;
Whose bashful elegance no brush can trace,
Heartfelt delight, and plenitude of grace ;
No palettes match their brilliance, although
Pandora filled her box from Iris' bow."

Pausias

" Her want of faith sweet Glycera will rue,
When she hath seen what *Pausias* can do."

Glycera

" Forgive me, sir ; In truth it was no taunt.
A great man can do anything—but vaunt."

Pausias

" E'en that he can do, if he sees the need.
But out on words, when time hath come for deed !
Up leaps the sun, to paint thee with his plume,
And every blossom seems to be thy bloom."

Glycera

" Why stand we here, so early of the morn,
In love with things that treat our love with scorn—
Grey crags, where Time with folded pinion broods,
And ever young antiquity of woods ;

The brooks that babble, and the flowers that blush,
Ere woman was a reed, or man a rush?
And he for ever, as the Gods ordain,
Would fain revive with art what he hath slain;
Shall nature fail to laugh, while man doth yearn
To teach the canvas what he ne'er can learn?"

Pausias

"Sweet Muse, while thus through heaven's too distant
vault,
Thy great mind roves—how shall we earn our salt?
Though art is not encouraged as of old,
    She is worth a score of nature; I design
    To manufacture, from these flowers of thine,
A silver* talent—or perhaps of gold!"

Glycera

"Good heavens, how precious is your Worship's time!
Some minds are lowly, others too sublime.
Before thee all my simple flowers I spread;
Long may they live, when Glycera is dead!"

Pausias

"The Gods forefend!   Fair omen from fair maid—
Bright tongue, recall the dark thing thou hast said!"

Glycera

"Then long live they, with Glycera to aid!"

* Lucullus is said to have given two talents for a mere copy of this picture.

Pausias
" Seven times the moon hath filled her silver horn,
And twice a hundred suns awoke the morn,
Since thou and I—for half the praise is thine—
Began this study of the flowers divine."

Glycera
" Alas ! how swiftly have the months gone by ! "

Pausias
" Not swift alone, but passing sweet for me."

Glycera
" The world, that was so large, is you and I."

Pausias
" And shall be larger still, when it is ' We.' "

Glycera
(Aside) " Sweet dual ! Alas, that this shall never be ! "

Pausias
" A tear, bright Glycera in those eyes of thine,
Those tender eyes, that should with triumph shine !
When I, the owner of that precious heart,
Am shouting Iö Pæan of high art ;
The noblest picture underneath the sun—
A few more strokes, and victory is won ! "

Glycera

" Nay, heed me not. True pleasure is not dry ;
The sunrise of the heart bedews the eye."

Pausias

" If that were all—but lately there hath been
A listless air beneath thy lively mien ;
Thyself art all fair petal, and sweet perfume,
And smiles that light the damask of thy bloom ;
Yet some pale distance seems to chill the whole."

Glycera

" Forgive me, love, forgive a timorous soul.
Through brightest hours untimely vapours rise—
But while I prate, the lucky moment flies.
The work, the weather, and the world are fair ;
A few more strokes—and fame flies everywhere."

Pausias

" Who cares for fame, except with love to share?"

Glycera

" To share ! Nay every breath of it is mine,
Whene'er it breathes on thee ; for I am thine.
But pardon now—if I have seemed sometime
Impatient, glib, too pert for things sublime,
Remember that I meant not so to sink ;
Forgive your Glycera, when you come to think."

Pausias
" I'll not forgive my Glycera—until
She hath discovered how to do some ill.
Now don once more this coronet of bloom,
While lilies sweet thy sweeter breast illume.

Glycera
(Aside) " Ah me, what brightness wasted upon gloom !
(Aloud) Oh fling thy sponge across this wretched face,
A patch uncouth amid a world of grace."

Pausias
" Sweet love, thy beauty far outshineth them ;
The tinsel they are, thou the living gem.
Great gift of Gods ! Shall flowers of earth despise
Those flowers of heaven—thy tresses, and thine eyes ?
Away with gloom ! let no ill-boding make
My heart to falter, or my hand to shake.
One hour is all I crave. If that be long,
Sweet lips beguile it with my favourite song."

Glycera
" A song like mine, a childish lullaby,
Will close—when needed wide-awake—thine eye.
But since thou so demandest, let me try.

" In the fresh woods have I been,
Sprinkled with the morning dew ;
And of all that I have seen,
Lo, the fairest are for you !

Take your choice of many a flower,
  Lily, rose, and melilot,
Lilac, myrtle, virgin's bower,
  Pansy, and forget-me-not.

Ladies'-tresses, and harebell,
  Jasmin, daphne, violet,
Meadow-sweet, and pimpernel,
  Maidenhair, and mignonette.

What is gold, that doth allure
  Foolish hearts from field and flower?
If you plant them in it pure,
  Will they keep alive an hour?

What is fame, compared with these,
  Fame of wisdom, sword, or pen?
Who would quit the meadow breeze,
  For the sultry breath of men?

These have been my childhood's love,
  These my maiden visions were;
When I meet their gaze above,
  These will tell me, God is there."

Pausias
" 'Tis done! No more the palsied doubt molests;
The crown of glory on my labour rests.
Thy clear voice hath my flagging thoughts supplied,
My model thou, my teacher, and my bride!
Now stand, beloved one, where the soft glow lies,
Yet judge not rashly, ere the colour dries.

Find every fault, pick every flaw thou canst;
I'll not be vexed; true art is thus advanced.
So meek is art, that (when it comprehends)
It loves the carping of its dearest friends.
If my own bride condemns my efforts—let her.
A poor daub? Well let some one do it better."

Glycera

" My love, my lord, my monarch of high art,
Forgive a tongue held fast and bound by heart.
Not Orpheus, Linus, or great Hermes could
Find words to make their rapture understood.
No Muse, no Phœbus, hath this work inspired,
But Jove himself, with heaven's own splendour fired.
I see the nursing fingers of the day,
And night as well, upon their offspring play—
The silent glide of moon, that hushed their sleep,
(As mother at her infant steals a peep)
Anon, with pearly glances half withdrawn,
The gentle hesitation of the dawn;
I see the sun his golden target raise,
And drive in tremulous ranks the woodland haze;
Awakened by whose call the flowers arise,
With tears of joy and blushes of surprise;
From bulb and bush, from leaf and blade, spring up
Bell, disk, or star, plume, sceptre, fan, or cup;
A thousand forms, a thousand hues of bloom
Fill earth and heaven with beauty and perfume.
All this, by thine enchantment, liveth here;
Oh wondrous power, that chills my pride with fear!"

Pausias

" Thy praise, sweet critic, makes thee doubly dear.
But what of thy fair self—thy form, thy face,
The flower of flowers, the gracefulness of grace?"

Glycera

" I see why thou hast placed me among these;
I serve a purpose—'tis to scare the bees.
Sweet love hath right to place me anywhere;
And yet I mourn, to find myself so fair."

Pausias

" A maid lament her beauty! Thou hast shown,
A thousand times, a wit beyond mine own;
Yet is it kind to such a love as mine,
To grudge it refuge in a lovely shrine?"

Glycera

" No shrine, no throne, of earth or heaven above,
Can be too fair a dwelling-place for love.
But that which makes me grieve, myself to see,
Is memory of the bitter loss to thee;
That earthly charms—as men such things esteem—
Should tantalize thee, in a weeping dream!"

Pausias

" My own, my only love, what wouldst thou say?
My heart hath borne a heavy bode, all day."

Glycera

" I durst not tell thee, till thy work was done ;
But now I must, before the setting sun.
Last night, when life was lapsed in quietude,
Beside my couch a stately figure stood—
A virgin form, in garb of chace arrayed,
With bow and quiver, baldric, and steel blade ;
Majestic as a palm that scorns the wind,
And taller than the daughters of mankind.
'Twas Artemis, close-girt in silver sheen,
The Goddess of the woods, the Maiden-queen.
Cold terror seized me, and mute awe, the while
She oped her proud lips, with an icy smile—
'Whose votary art thou ? Shall I resign
'To wanton Cypris this sworn nymph of mine ?
'Have I enfeoffed thee of my holiest glen,
'To have thee tainted by the lips of men ?
'Shall urchin Eros laugh at my decree ?
'No Hymen torch, no loosened zone for thee !
'To-morrow, when my crescent tops yon oak,
'Thou shalt return unto thy proper yoke.'
She closed her lips, and like the barb of frost,
    Her fingers on my bounding heart outspread :
    My breast is ice, my soul is of the dead :
    The sod, the cold clay, are my marriage-bed ;
Sweet sun, sweet flowers, sweet Love, for ever lost ! "

Pausias

" I'll not endure it ; it shall ne'er be true ;
If that cold tyrant comes—I'll run her through."

BUSCOMBE; OR, A MICHAELMAS GOOSE

HEN I was Head of Blundell's
    school,
  Before the age of stokers,
Compelled by rank to look a fool
  Betwixt a pair of " chokers,"

Tom Tanner's father's wrote, to
    say
That we should both of us come,
To spend Saint Michael's holiday
  At the Vicarage of Buscombe.

One trifle marred this merry plan—
  I had contrived, though barr'd up,
To typify the future man,
  By getting very hard up.

113   q

Oh bimetallic champion, some
　New ratio doth seem proper,
When the circulating medium
　Has fallen to half a copper.

Vile mammon hence! Thy low amount
　Too paltry is to mope for;
The more we have in hand to count,
　The less in heart to hope for.

Bright youth itself is golden ore,
　And health the best gold-beater:
Without a sigh for two pence more,
　We passed the gates of Peter.

A nod suffices surly Cop,
　Who grins his *bona fides*;
As Cerberus preferred his sop
　To Orpheus and Alcides.

But Mother Cop! Her cooking knack
　Would conquer fifty Catos—
The Queen of tarts, and tuck, and tack,
　And cream, and fried potatoes.

And rashers! Sweet Ulysses, say
　Old Homer was mistaken;
The Goddess must have had her way,
　And turned thee into bacon.

That Circe came, and wished us joy,
   And said, " Goodbye, my dearie ! "
Because I was an honest boy,
   And *pauper meo ære.*

So Tom and I, like men on strike,
   Shook hands with all our cronies,
Walked fifty yards, to save the pike,
   And jumped upon our ponies.

Of apples, nuts, and goose galore
   I chattered, like a stupid,
And thought of shooting coneys, more
   Than being shot by Cupid.

    *   *   *   *

At racing pace the turnpike road
   (Great Western, in this quicker age)
Was swallowed up with whip and goad,
   And soon we saw the Vicarage.

A sweet seclusion, to forget
   The world and its disasters,
And fill the mind with mignonette,
   Clove-pinks, and German asters ;

In pensive, or in playful mood,
   To saunter here, and dally
With leafy calm of solitude,
   Or sunshine of the valley.

The Vicar loved his parish well,
    And well was he loved by it ;
Religion did not him compel
    To harass and defy it.

No price he charged for Heavenly love,
    No discount on *Resurgo ;*
His conscience told him—one side-shove
    Is worth ten kicks *a tergo.*

But while the path of life he showed
    To win the Christian guerdon,
No post was he, to point the road,
    But a man to share the burden.

The lapse of years made manifest
    The sanctuary of holy age ;
As clearer grows the ring-dove's nest,
    When time hath stripp'd the foliage.

The Vicar's wife was much the same,
    In fairer form presented—
A lively, yet a quiet dame,
    With home, sweet home, contented.

In parish needs, and household arts,
    A lesson to this glib age ;
Well versed in pickles, jams, and tarts,
    Piano, chess, and cribbage.

And well she loved the flowers, that speak
 A language undefiléd—
The flowers that lift the dimpled cheek,
 Or droop the dewy eyelid.

    *   *   *   *

Now, if she lingers after us,
 What ground have we for snarling?
What act prohibits private buss,
 Reserved for "Tommy darling"?

    *   *   *   *

But who are these, so fresh and sweet,
 In lovely hats and dresses,
Who half advance, and half retreat,
 And peep through clouds of tresses?

"Come, dears!" They shyly offer hand,
 Beneath the jasmin trellis;
"Say who you are, girls"—Charlotte, and
 Her sister, Caroline Ellis!

Sweet Charlotte hath a serious face,
 A gaze almost parental;
A type of every maiden grace,
 But a wee bit sentimental.

Bright Caroline hath eyes that dance,
 While buoyant airs engirdle her;
Her playful soul may love romance,
 But not a creepy curdler.

Sweet Charlotte's are the deep grey eyes
That win profound devotion ;
Bright Carry's flash, like azure skies,
With heliograph in motion.

As merry as the vintage ray,
That dances down the grape-rill ;
As tender as the dews of May,
Or apple-buds of April.

Their charms are safe to grow more bright
For at least two lustral stages ;
And so it seems not unpolite
To enquire what their age is.

" Last May, I was fifteen"; with glee
Replies the laughing Carry ;
Sage Charlotte adds—"And I shall be
Seventeen, next February."

To the dining-room we walk on air,
Disdaining jots and tittles ;
To feed seems such a low affair—
And yet, hurrah for victuals !

Could e'en a boy ply knife and fork,
In presence so poetic,
Until the vicar draws a cork,
And gives the sniff prophetic ?

118

And when the evening games began,
   Pope Joan, and Speculation—
What head could keep its poise and plan,
   With the heart in palpitation?

Until, in soft white-curtained bed,
   We sink to slumber lowly,
And angels fan the childish head,
   With visions sweet and holy.

* * * *

" Now I do declare," exclaimed our host,
   As he strode back from the arish,
" Those railway fellows soon will boast
   They have undermined my parish!

" Though none can say I have ever set
   My face against improvement,
I cannot quite perceive as yet
   The good of this new movement.

" Like Hannibal, these folk confound
   All nature's institutions,
And shun, with a great dive underground,
   Parochial contributions!

" Come boys and girls, let us see their craft,
   These hills of Devon will task it;
'Tis a pretty walk to White-Ball shaft,
   If the boys will take a basket.

119

" Dear wife, if your poor feet are right,
    The miracles of this cycle
Will give you a noble appetite,
    For the roast goose of Saint Michael."

In a twinkle, we had baskets twain
    Of the right stuff for a journey,
And beautiful gooseberry Champagne,
    Superior to Epernay.

      *   *   *   *

What myriad joys of heart and mind
    Flit in and out our brief age!
That day it was grand to see how kind
    The sun looked through the leafage!

While the leaves for their part pricked their
        lips,
    With a dewy simper waiting;
They were conscious of some amber tips—
    But those were his own creating.

Can the heart of man alone be dull,
    And the mind of man be spiteful,
When all above is beautiful,
    And all below delightful?

When Season bright, and Season rich,
    Make bids against each other;
And earth, uncertain which is which,
    Smiles up at Nature Mother.

The copse, the lane, the meadow path,
  The valleys, banks, and hedges,
Were green with summer's aftermath,
  And gold with autumn's pledges.

Wild rose hung coral beads above,
  And satchel'd nuts grew nigh them ;
Like tips of a little maiden's glove,
  Ere ever she has to buy them.

      *   *   *   *

But ours are not the maids to bite
  A gore or gusset undone ;
How neat they look, how trim and tight !
  Those frocks were made in London.

Long time, we glance in awe and doubt,
  Suppressing all frivolity ;
Till the spirit of the age breaks out,
  And all is mirth and jollity.

One flash, that stole from eyes demure,
  Hath scattered all convention ;
And then a pearly laugh makes sure
  That fun is her intention.

The smiling elders march ahead ;
  We dance, without a fiddler,
We play at cross-touch, White and Red,
  Tip-cat, and Tommy Tidler.

We laugh and shout, much more than speak,
  No etiquette importunes ;
The trees were made for hide-and-seek,
  The flowers to tell our fortunes ;

The hills, for pretty girls to pant,
  And glow with richer roses ;
The wind itself, to toss askant
  The curls that hide their noses.

Then sprightly Carry shouts in French—
  "All boys and girls, come nutting ! "
We are slipping down a mighty trench—
  Why, it is the Railway cutting !

Before us yawns a dark-browed arch,
  Paved with a muddy runnel ;
A thousand giant navvies march
  To delve the White-Ball tunnel.

Oh, if a man of them but did
  Presume to glance at Carry,
Though he were Milo, or John Ridd,
  I would toss him to Old Harry.

I pull my jacket off, like him
  Who would shatter England's pillars—
From the tunnel comes an order grim,
  "Get out of the way you chil'lers ! "

          *   *   *   *

And the same stern order doth apply
  To the pranks of this remote age;
We are sure alike to be thrust by,
  In our nonage, and our dotage.

Yet who shall grudge the tranquil age,
  When nought can now betide ill,
To glance, from a distant hermitage,
  At a summer morning idyll?

  * * * *

Oh agony, despair, and woe!
  Oh two-edged sword to us come!
To Blundell's must the body go,
  While the heart remains at Buscombe.

All breakfast time, how glum we looked!
  Our tears were threatening dribblets;
Too truly had our goose been cooked,
  To leave us e'en our giblets.

Sweet Charlotte, did you share the thrill,
  The pang no throat may utter,
And strive an aching void to fill
  With heartless toast and butter?

And were you sad, bright Caroline,
  Although you never said so?
You did cast down your lovely eyne,
  And you crumbled up your bread so!

But the Vicar's views were more sublime,
  As he asked in all simplicity,
" My youthful friends, what is the prime
  Of all mundane felicity?"

My answer, though it sounded cool,
  Was given with trepidation—
" To stay at home, and send to school
  The rising generation."

A gentle smile flits o'er his lip,
  He eyes me with benignity;
He yearns to offer goodly tip,
  Yet fears to wound my dignity.

True benefactor, be not shy,
  Thou seest a humble fellow,
Thy noble impulse gratify—
  My stars, if it isn't yellow!

* * * *

But time is over, and above,
  To end this charming visit;
And must we part my own true love?
  Though I am not sure, which is it.

Sweet Charlotte lingered in the shade,
  Most gentle of all houris;
Bright Carry in the lobby played
  With a pair of polished cowries.

124

She showed me how alike they were,
  So Heaven had pleased to make them.
Though fortune might divide the pair,
  She ne'er could separate them.

I blushed, and stammered at her touch,
  I feared to beg for either;
My heart was in my mouth so much,
  I could say " Goodbye" to neither.

     *   *   *   *

Two strings are wise for every bow,
  To meet the change of weather;
And Cupid's shafts give softer blow,
  When two are tied together.

Oh, Charlotte sweet, and Carry bright,
  My whole, or double-half love,
Let no maturer wisdom slight
  A simple tale of calf-love.

A blessing on the maiden grace,
  That beautifies the real,
To make the world a fairer place,
  And lift the low ideal!

If one, or both, by any chance,
  Behold what I confess here,
Make auld lang syne of young romance,
  By sending your address here.

TO FAME

I

RIGHT Fairy of the morn, with
flowers arrayed,
Whose beauties to thy young
pursuer seem
Beyond the ecstasy of poet's
dream—
Shall I o'ertake thee, ere thy
lustre fade?

II

Ripe glory of the noon, august, and proud,
A vision of high purpose, power, and skill,
That melteth into mirage of good-will—
Do I o'ertake thee, or embrace a cloud?

III

Gray shadow of the evening, gaunt and bare,
At random cast, beyond me or above,
And cold as memory in the arms of love—
If I o'ertook thee now, what should I care?

IV

"No morn, or noon, or eve am I," she said ;
  "But night—the depth of night behind the sun ;
    By all mankind pursued ; but never won,
Until my shadow falls upon a shade."

1894.

List of Books
in
Belles Lettres

ALL THE BOOKS IN THIS CATALOGUE ARE
PUBLISHED AT NET PRICES

London : Elkin Mathews, Vigo Street, W.

1895

Telegraphic Address—
'ELEGANTIA, LONDON.'

Lector ! eme, lege, & gaudebis

List of Books

IN

BELLES LETTRES

(Including some Transfers)

PUBLISHED BY

ELKIN MATHEWS

VIGO STREET, LONDON, W.

N.B.—The Authors and Publisher reserve the right of reprinting any book in this list, except in cases where a stipulation has been made to the contrary, and of printing a separate edition of any of the books for America. In the case of limited Editions, the numbers mentioned do not include the copies sent for review, nor those supplied to the public libraries. The prices of books not yet published are subject to variation.

The Books mentioned in this Catalogue can be obtained to order by any Bookseller. It should be noted also that they are supplied to the Trade on terms which will not allow of discount.

◆§§◆

The following are a few of the Authors represented in this Catalogue :

P. ADDLESHAW.	LIONEL JOHNSON.
R. D. BLACKMORE.	CHARLES LAMB.
F. W. BOURDILLON.	RICHARD LE GALLIENNE.
BLISS CARMAN.	P. B. MARSTON.
E. R. CHAPMAN.	HON. RODEN NOEL.
ERNEST DOWSON.	MAY PROBYN.
MICHAEL FIELD.	F. YORK POWELL.
T. GORDON HAKE.	J. A. SYMONDS.
ARTHUR HALLAM.	JOHN TODHUNTER.
KATHARINE HINKSON.	HENRY VAN DYKE.
HERBERT P. HORNE.	THEODORE WATTS.
RICHARD HOVEY.	FREDERICK WEDMORE.
LEIGH HUNT.	P. H. WICKSTEED.
SELWYN IMAGE.	W. B. YEATS.

ABBOTT (DR. C. C.).

TRAVELS IN A TREE-TOP.   Sm. 8vo.   5s. net.
Philadelphia : J. B. Lippincott Company.

"Dr. Abbott pleases by the interest he takes in the subject which he treats . . and he adorns his matter with a good English style . . . Altogether, with its dainty printing, it would be a charming book to read in the open air on a bright summer's day.—*Athenæum.*

"He has an observant eye, a warm sympathy, and a pen that enables us to see with him. Nothing could be more restful than to read the thoughts of such nature-lovers. The very titles of his chapters suggest quiet and gentle things."—*Dublin Herald.*

"A delightful volume this of Nature Sketches. Dr. Abbott writes about New England woods and streams, scenes neither quite familiar nor quite strange to us who know the same things in the old country. The severer winter makes some difference, as, for instance, in the number of birds that migrate there, but are stationary here; and there are, of course, other differences in both fauna and flora; nevertheless, we feel, in a way, at home, when Dr. Abbott takes us on one of his delightful winter or summer excursions. This is a book which we cannot recommend too highly."—*Spectator.*

THE BIRDS ABOUT US.   73 Engravings.   Second Edition.
Thick cr. 8vo.   5s. 6d. net.

Philadelphia : J. B. Lippincott Company.

BATEMAN (MAY).

A VOLUME OF POEMS.   With a title design by P. WILSON
STEER.   [*Shortly.*

BINYON (LAURENCE).

LYRIC POEMS, with title page by SELWYN IMAGE.   Sq.
16mo.   5s. net.

"This little volume of LYRIC POEMS displays a grace of fancy, a spontaneity and individuality of inspiration, and a felicitous command of metre and diction, which lift the writer above the average of the minor singers of our time. . . . We may expect much from the writer of 'An April Day,' or of the strong concluding lines on the present age from a piece entitled 'Present and Future.' "—*Times.*

"The product of a definite and sympathetic personality."—*Globe.*

"The impression that this volume makes upon us is that the writer has caught the spirit of Matthew Arnold, and that in no common degree. . . . Quite Titianesque in its force and colour."—*Spectator.*

BLACKMORE (R. D.)

FRINGILLA : OR, SOME TALES IN VERSE.   By the Author
of "Lorna Doone."   With Eleven full-page Illustrations
and numerous vignettes and initials by LOUIS FAIRFAX-
MUCKLEY and Three by JAMES W. R. LINTON.
Crown 8vo.   10s. net.

*(Quorsum haec ?   Non potui qualem Philomela querelam ; Sed
fringilla velut pipitabunda, vagor.)*

BLACKMORE (R. D.)—continued.

. . . "This volume of poems, with its fantastic title, is one of the literary events of the hour."—*Queen.*

"Mr. Blackmore, the novelist, has always been known among his friends as poet and scholar too. The first book he published, at the age of thirty-two, was a translation of the first two books of the 'Georgics.' That was seven years before he wrote ' Lorna Doone,' which made him famous. He is now about to appeal to the public as poet on his own account with a book of Tales in Verse, entitled ' Fringilla.' . . . Some day perhaps he will give us some Georgics of his own, informed and inspired by the experience, insight, and affections gained as a market-gardener now of considerable standing.'—*St. James's Gazette.*

BOURCHIER (MARIA).

SUMMER SNOWS : A TALE.   [*In preparation.*

BOURDILLON (F. W.).

A LOST GOD : a Poem in Three Books. With illustrations by H. J. FORD. Printed at the CHISWICK PRESS. 500 copies. 8vo. 6s. *net.*   [*Very few remain.* Also 50 copies, royal 8vo., L.P. 17s. 6d. *net.*

" A graceful presentation in blank verse, with slight but effective dramatic setting, of the legend of the death of Pan on the morning that Christ began his teaching."—*Times.*

[Isham Facsimile Reprint.]

BRETON (NICHOLAS).

No WHIPPINGE, NOR TRIPPINGE, BUT A KINDE FRIENDLY SNIPPINGE. London, 1601. A Facsimile Reprint, with the original Borders to every page, with a Bibliographical Note by CHARLES EDMONDS. 200 copies, printed on hand-made paper at the CHISWICK PRESS. 12mo. 3s. 6d. *net.* Also 50 copies Large Paper. 5s. *net.*

Facsimile reprint from the semi-unique copy discovered in the autumn of 1867 by Mr. Charles Edmonds in a disused lumber room at Lamport Hall, Northants (Sir Charles E. Isham's), and purchased lately by the British Museum authorities. When Dr. A. B. Grosart collected Breton's Works a few years ago for his " Chertsey Worthies Library," he was forced to confess that certain of Breton's most coveted books were missing and absolutely unavailable. The semi-unique example under notice was one of these.

CARMAN (BLISS) & RICHARD HOVEY.

SONGS FROM VAGABONDIA. With Decorations by TOM B. METEYARD. Fcap. 8vo. 5s. *net.*

Boston : Copeland & Day.

" The Authors of the small joint volume called ' Songs from Vagabondia,' have an unmistakable right to the name of poet. These little snatches have the spirit of a

CARMAN (BLISS) &· RICHARD HOVEY—continued.

gipsy Omar Khayyám. They have always careless verve, and often careless felicity; they are masculine and rough, as roving songs should be. . . . Here, certainly, is the poet's soul. . . . You have the whole spirit of the book in such an unforgetable little lyric as ' In the House of Idledally.' . . . We refer the reader to the delightful little volume itself, which comes as a welcome interlude amidst the highly wrought introspective poetry of the day."—FRANCIS THOMPSON, in *Merry England.*

" Bliss Carman is the author of a delightful volume of verse, ' Low Tide on Grand Pré,' and Richard Hovey is the foremost of the living poets of America, with the exception, perhaps, of Bret Harte and Joaquin Miller, whose names are more familiar. He sounds a deeper note than either of these, and deals with loftier themes."—*Dublin Express.*

" Both possess the power of investing actualities with fancy, and leaving them none the less actual; of setting the march music of the vagabond's feet to words; of being comrades with nature, yet without presumption. And they have that charm, rare in writers of verse, of drawing the reader into the fellowship of their own zest and contentment."—*Athenæum.*

CHAPMAN (ELIZABETH RACHEL).

A LITTLE CHILD'S WREATH : A Sonnet Sequence. With title page and cover designed by SELWYN IMAGE. Second Edition. Sq. 16mo., green buckram. 3s. 6d. net. *New York: Dodd, Mead &· Company.*

" Contains many tender and pathetic passages, and some really exquisite and subtle touches of childhood nature. . . . The average excellence of the sonnets is undoubted."—*Spectator.*

" In these forty pages of poetry . . . we have a contribution inspired by grief for the loss of a child of seven, which is not unworthy to take its place even beside ' In Memoriam.' . . . Miss Chapman has ventured upon sacred ground, but she has come off safely, with the inspiration of a divine sympathy in her soul, and with lips touched with the live coal from the altar on which glows th flame of immortal love "—W. T. STEAD, in *The Review of Reviews.*

" Full of a very solemn and beautiful but never exaggerated sentiment.'—LOGROLLER, in *Star.*

" While they are brimming with tenderness and tears, they are marked witht skilled workmanship of the real poet."—*Glasgow Herald.*

" Evidently describes very real and intense sorrow. Its strains of tender sympathy will appeal specially to those whose hearts have been wrong by the loss of a young child, and the verses are touching in their simplicity "—*Morning Post.*

" Re-assures us on its first page by its sanity and its simple tenderness."—*Bookman.*

COLERIDGE (HON. STEPHEN).

THE SANCTITY OF CONFESSION : A Romance. 2nd edition. Printed by CLOWES & SON. 250 copies. Cr. 8vo. 3s. net.   [*Very few remain.*

" Mr. Stephen Coleridge's sixteenth-century romance is well and pleasantly written. The style is throughout in keeping with the story; and we should imagine that the historical probabilities are well observed."—*Pall Mall Gazette.*

Mr. GLADSTONE writes :—"I have read the singularly well told story. . . . It opens up questions both deep and dark; it cannot be right to accept in religion or anything else a secret which destroys the life of an innocent fellow creature."

CORBIN (JOHN).
THE ELIZABETHAN HAMLET: A Study of the Sources,
and of Shakspere's Environment, to show that the Mad
Scenes had a Comic Aspect now Ignored. With a
Prefatory Note by F. YORK POWELL, Professor of
Modern History at the University of Oxford. Small
4to. 3s. 6d. net.
New York: Charles Scribner's Sons.

This book is a study of the sources of "Hamlet," and of Shakespeare's environment, with the object of showing that the mad scenes in the play had a comic
aspect now ignored. Mr. Corbin's general standpoint is that Shakespeare naturally
wrote the drama for Elizabethan audiences. They in their time saw jest in what
would seem to us only the severest tragedy. What he wishes to get at is the comedy
in "Hamlet" according to the Elizabethan point of view.
. . . "When we add that so competent a judge as Professor York Powell
expresses his belief in a Prefatory Note that Mr. Corbin has 'got hold of a truth that
has not been clearly, if at all, expressed in our Elizabethan studies—to wit, that the
16th century audience's point of view, and, of necessity, the playwright's treatment
of his subject, were very different from ours of to-day in many matters of mark'—and
express our own concurrence in this, we have said enough to recommend Mr. Corbin's
little book to the attention of all Shakespearian students."—Times.

CROSSING (WILLIAM).
THE ANCIENT CROSSES OF DARTMOOR; with a Description of their Surroundings. With 11 plates. 8vo. cloth.
4s. 6d. net.   [Very few remain.

DAVIES (R. R.).
SOME ACCOUNT OF THE OLD CHURCH AT CHELSEA AND
OF ITS MONUMENTS.   [In preparation.

DE GRUCHY (AUGUSTA).
UNDER THE HAWTHORN, AND OTHER VERSES. With
Frontispiece by WALTER CRANE. Printed at the
RUGBY PRESS. 300 copies. Cr. 8vo. 5s. net.
Also 30 copies on Japanese vellum. 15s. net.

"Melodious in metre, graceful in fancy, and not without spontaneity of inspiration."—Times.
"Very tender and melodious is much of Mrs. De Gruchy's verse. Rare imaginative
power marks the dramatic monologue ' In the Prison Van.' "—Speaker.
"Distinguished by the attractive qualities of grace and refinement, and a purity
of style that is as refreshing as a limpid stream in the heat of a summer's noon. . . .
The charm of these poems lies in their naturalness, which is indeed an admirable
quality in song."—Saturday Review.

DESTRÉE (OLIVIER GEORGES).
POÈMES SANS RIMES. Imprimé à Londres aux Presses de
Chiswick, d'apres les dessins de HERBERT P. HORNE.
25 copies for sale. Square cr. 8vo. 8s. 6d. net.

DIVERSI COLORES SERIES.
See HORNE.

DOWSON (ERNEST).

DILEMMAS : Stories and Studies in Sentiment. (A Case of
Conscience.—The Diary of a Successful Man.—An
Orchestral Violin.—The Statute of Limitations.—
Souvenirs of an Egoist). Crown 8vo. 3s. 6d. *net.*

POEMS (*Diversi Colores* Series). With a title design by
H. P. HORNE. Printed at the CHISWICK PRESS, on
hand-made paper. 16mo. 5s. *net.* [*Shortly.*

"Mr. Dowson's contributions to the two series of the *Rhymer's Book* were
subtle and exquisite poems. He has a touch of Elizabethan distinction. . . .
Mr. Dowson's stories are very remarkable in quality."—*Boston Literary World.*

FIELD (MICHAEL).

SIGHT AND SONG (Poems on Pictures). Printed by
CONSTABLES. 400 copies. 12mo. 5s. *net.*
[*Very few remain.*

"This is a fascinating little volume; one that will give to many readers a
new interest in the examples of pictorial art with which it deals. Certainly, in the
delight in the beauty of the human form, and of the fair shows of earth, and sea,
and sky which it manifests, and in the harmonious verbal expression which this
delight has found, the book is one of the most Keats-like things that has been
produced since Keats himself took his seat among the immortals."—*Academy.*

"The verses have a sober grace and harmony, and the truth and poetic delicacy
of the work is only realised on a close comparison with the picture itself. It is
soothing and pleasant to participate in such leisurely degustation and enjoyment, such
insistent penetration, for these poems are far removed from mere description, and the
renderings, though somewhat lacking in the sense of humour, show both courage and
poetical imagination."—*Westminster Review.*

STEPHANIA : A TRIALOGUE IN THREE ACTS. Frontispiece, colophon, and ornament for binding designed
by SELWYN IMAGE. Printed by FOLKARD & SON.
250 copies (200 for sale). Pott 4to. 6s. *net.*
[*Very few remain.*

"We have true drama in 'Stephania.' . . . . Stephania, Otho, and
Sylvester II., the three persons of the play, are more than mere names. . . . .
Besides great effort, commendable effort, there is real greatness in this play ; and the
blank verse is often sinewy and strong with thought and passion."—*Speaker.*

"'Stephania' is striking in design and powerful in execution. It is a highly
dramatic 'trialogue' between the Emperor Otho III., his tutor Gerbert, and Stephania,
the widow of the murdered Roman Consul, Crescentius. The poem contains much
fine work, and is picturesque and of poetical accent. . ."—*Westminster Review.*

A QUESTION OF MEMORY : A PLAY IN FOUR ACTS.
100 copies only. 8vo. 5s. *net.* [*Very few remain.*

GALTON (ARTHUR).
ESSAYS UPON MATTHEW ARNOLD (*Diversi Colores* Series).
Printed at the CHISWICK PRESS on hand-made paper.
Cr. 8vo.   5s. net.   [*In preparation.*

GASKIN (MRS. ARTHUR).
AN A.B.C. BOOK.   Rhymed and Pictured by MRS.
ARTHUR GASKIN.   [*In preparation.*

HAKE (DR. T. GORDON, "The Parable Poet.")
MADELINE, AND OTHER POEMS.   Crown 8vo.   5s. net.
                              Transferred to the present Publisher.

"The ministry of the angel Daphne to her erring human sister is frequently
related in strains of pure and elevated tenderness. Nor does the poet who can show
so much delicacy fall in strength. The description of Madeline as she passes in
trance to her vengeance is full of vivid pictures and charged with tragic feeling.
The individuality of the writer lies in his deep sympathy with whatever affects the
being and condition of man. . . . Taken as a whole, the book has high and
unusual claims."—*Athenæum.*

"I have been reading 'Madeline' again. For sheer originality, both of conception
and of treatment, I consider that it stands alone."—MR. THEODORE WATTS.

PARABLES AND TALES. (Mother and Child.—The Crip-
ple.—The Blind Boy.—Old Morality.—Old Souls.—
The Lily of the Valley.—The Deadly Nightshade.—
The Poet). With a Biographical Sketch by THEODORE
WATTS.   9 illustrations by ARTHUR HUGHES.   New
Edition.   Crown 8vo.   3s. 6d. net.

"The qualities of Dr. Gordon Hake's work were from the first fully admitted
and warmly praised by one of the greatest of contemporary poets, who was also a
critic of exceptional acuteness—Rossetti. Indeed, the only two review articles which
Rossetti ever wrote were written on two of Dr. Hake's books: 'Madeline,' which he
reviewed in the *Academy* in 1871, and 'Parables and Tales,' which he reviewed in
the *Fortnightly* in 1873. Many eminent critics have expressed a decided preference
for 'Parables and Tales' to Dr. Hake's other works, and it had the advantage of being
enriched with the admirable illustrations of Arthur Hughes."—*Saturday Review,*
January, 1895.

"The piece called 'Old Souls' is probably secure of a distinct place in the literature of our day, and we believe the same may be predicted of other poems in the
little collection just issued. . . . Should Dr. Hake's more restricted, but lovely
and sincere contributions to the poetry of real life not find the immediate response
they deserve, he may at least remember that others also have failed to meet at once
with full justice and recognition. But we will hope for good encouragement to his
present and future work; and can at least ensure the lover of poetry that in these
simple pages he shall find not seldom a humanity limpid and pellucid—the well-spring
of a true heart, with which his tears must mingle as with their own element.

"Dr. Hake has been fortunate in the beautiful drawings which Mr. Arthur
Hughes has contributed to his little volume. No poet could have a more congenial
yoke-fellow than this gifted and imaginative artist."—D. G. ROSSETTI, in the
Fortnightly, 1873.

HALLAM (ARTHUR).

THE POEMS OF ARTHUR HENRY HALLAM, together with his Essay "ON SOME OF THE CHARACTERISTICS OF MODERN POETRY, AND ON THE LYRICAL POEMS OF ALFRED TENNYSON," reprinted from the *Englishman's Magazine*, 1831, edited, with an introduction, by RICHARD LE GALLIENNE. 550 copies (500 for sale). Small 8vo. 5s. net.

New York: Macmillan & Co.

Many of these Poems are of great Tennysonian interest, having been addressed to Alfred, Charles, and Emily Tennyson.

HAMILTON (COL. IAN).

THE BALLAD OF HADJI, AND OTHER POEMS. With etched frontispiece by WILLIAM STRANG. Printed at the CHISWICK PRESS. 550 copies. 12mo. 3s. net.

Transferred by the Author to the present Publisher.

" Here is a dainty volume of clear, sparkling verse. The thought is sparkling, and the lines limpid and lightly flowing."—*Scotsman.*

HARPER (CHARLES G.)

REVOLTED WOMAN: PAST, PRESENT, AND TO COME. Printed by STRANGEWAYS. Illustrated with numerous original drawings and facsimiles by the Author. Crown 8vo. 5s. net.

" Mr. Harper, like a modern John Knox, denounces the monstrous regiment of women, making the ' New Woman ' the text of a discourse that bristles with historical instances and present day portraits."—*Saturday Review.*
" The illustrations are distinctly clever."—*Publishers' Circular.*

HEMINGWAY (PERCY).

OUT OF EGYPT: Stories from the Threshold of the East. Cover design by GLEESON WHITE. Crown 8vo. 3s. 6d. net.

" This is a strong book."—*Academy.*
" This is a remarkable book. Egyptian life has seldom been portrayed from the Inside. . . . The author's knowledge of Arabic, his sympathy with the religion of Islam, above all his entire freedom from Western prejudice, have enabled him to learn more of what modern Egypt really is than the average Englishman could possibly acquire in a lifetime at Cairo or Port Said."—*African Review.*
" A lively and picturesque style. . . . undoubted talent."—*Manchester Guardian.*
" But seldom that the first production o. an author is so mature and so finished in style as this. . . . The sketches are veritable spoils of the Egyptians—gems of prose in a setting of clear air, sharp outlines, and wondrous skies.—*Morning Leader.*

HEMINGWAY (PERCY)—continued.

"This book places its author amongst those writers from whom lasting work of high aim is to be expected."—*The Star.*

"The tale . . . is treated with daring directness. . . An impressive and pathetic close to a story told throughout with arresting strength and simplicity."—*Daily News.*

"Genuine power and pathos."—*Pall Mall Gazette.*

THE HAPPY WANDERER (Poems). With title design by Charles I. ffoulkes. Printed at the CHISWICK PRESS, on hand-made paper. Sq. 16mo. 5s. net.   [*In the press.*

HICKEY (EMILY H.).

A VOLUME OF POEMS.   [*In preparation.*

VERSE TALES, LYRICS AND TRANSLATIONS. Printed at the ARNOLD PRESS. 300 copies. Imp. 16mo. 5s. net.   [*Very few remain.*

'Miss Hickey's 'Verse Tales, Lyrics, and Translations' almost invariably reach a high level of finish and completeness. The book is a string of little rounded pearls.—*Athenæum.*

HINKSON (HENRY A.).

DUBLIN VERSES. By MEMBERS OF TRINITY COLLEGE. Selected and Edited by H. A. HINKSON, late Scholar of Trinity College, Dublin. Pott 4to. 5s. net. *Dublin: Hodges, Figgis & Co., Limited.*

Includes contributions by the following :—Aubrey de Vere, Sir Stephen de Vere, Oscar Wilde, J. K. Ingram, A. P. Graves, J. Todhunter, W. E. H. Lecky, T. W. Rolleston, Edward Dowden, G. A. Greene, Savage-Armstrong, Douglas Hyde, R. Y. Tyrrell, G. N. Plunkett, W. Macneile Dixon, William Wilkins, George Wilkins, and Edwin Hamilton.

"A pleasant volume of contemporary Irish Verse. . . A judicious selection." —*Times.*

"Wherever there is a group of Irish readers in near or far-off lands, these 'Dublin Verses' will be sure to command attention and applause."—*Glasgow Herald.*

HINKSON (KATHARINE).

SLOES ON THE BLACKTHORN: A VOLUME OF IRISH STORIES. Crown 8vo., 3s. 6d. net.   [*In preparation.*

"HOBBY HORSE (THE)."

AN ILLUSTRATED ART MISCELLANY. Edited by HERBERT P. HORNE. The Fourth Number of the New Series will shortly appear, after which MR. MATHEWS will publish all the numbers in a volume, price £1. 1s. net. *Boston: Copeland & Day.*

HORNE (HERBERT P.)

DIVERSI COLORES: Poems, Vignette, &c., designed by
the Author. Printed at the CHISWICK PRESS. 250
copies. 16mo. 5s. net.

Transferred by the Author to the present Publisher.

" In these few poems Mr. Horne has set before a tasteless age, and an extravagant
age, examples of poetry which, without fear or hesitation, we consider to be of true
and pure beauty."—*Anti-Jacobin.*

" With all his fondness for sixteenth century styles and themes, Mr. Horne is yet
sufficiently individual in his thought and manner. Much of his sentiment is quite
latter-day in tone and rendering ; he is a child of his time."—*Globe.*

" Mr. Horne's work is almost always carefully felicitous and may be compared
with beautiful filagree work in verse. He is fully, perhaps too fully, conscious of the
value of restraint, and is certainly in need of no more culture in the handling of verse
—of such verse as alone he cares to work in. He has already the merits of a finished
artist—or, at all events, of an artist who is capable of the utmost finish."—*Pall
Mall Gazette.*

The SERIES OF BOOKS begun in "DIVERSI COLORES" by
Mr. HERBERT P. HORNE, will continue to be published by Mr. Elkin Mathews.

The intention of the series is to give, in a collected and
sometimes revised form, Poems and Essays by various
writers, whose names have hitherto been chiefly asso-
ciated with the *Hobby Horse.* The series will be edited
by Mr. HERBERT P. Horne, and will contain :

No. II. POEMS AND CAROLS. By SELWYN IMAGE.
[*Just published.*

No. III. ESSAYS UPON MATTHEW ARNOLD. By AR-
THUR GALTON. [*Immediately.*

No. IV. POEMS. By ERNEST DOWSON.

No. V. THE LETTERS AND PAPERS OF ADAM LE-
GENDRE.

Each volume will contain a new title-page and ornaments
designed by the Editor ; and the volumes of verse will be
uniform with "Diversi Colores."

HORTON (ALICE).

POEMS.   [*Shortly.*

HUEFFER (OLIVER F. MADOX).

SONNETS AND POEMS. With a frontispiece.   [*Shortly.*

HUGHES (ARTHUR).
    See HAKE.

HUNT (LEIGH).
    A VOLUME OF ESSAYS now collected for the first time.
    Edited with a critical Introduction by R. W. M.
    JOHNSON.   [*In the press.*

IMAGE (SELWYN).
    POEMS AND CAROLS. (*Diversi Colores* Series.—New
    Volume). Title design by H. P. HORNE. Printed
    on hand-made paper at the CHISWICK PRESS. 16mo.
    5s. net.   [*Just ready.*
    " Among the artists who have turned poets will shortly have to be reckoned Mr.
Selwyn Image. A volume of poems from his pen will be published by Mr. Elkin
Mathews before long. Those who are acquainted with Mr. Selwyn Image's work
will expect to find a real and deep poetic charm in this book."—*Daily Chronicle.*
    " No one else could have done it (*i.e.*, written ' Poems and Carols ') in just this
way, and the artist himself could have done it in no other way."   " A remarkable
impress of personality, and this personality of singular rarity and interest. Every
piece is perfectly composed ; the ' mental cartooning,' to use Rossetti's phrase, has
been adequately done . . . an air of grave and homely order . . . a union of
quaint and subtly simple homeliness, with a somewhat abstract severity. . . . It
is a new thing, the revelation of a new poet. . . . Here is a book which may be
trusted to outlive most contemporary literature."—*Saturday Review.*
    " An intensely personal expression of a personality of singular charm, gravity,
fancifulness, and interest ; work which is alone among contemporary verse alike in
regard to substance and to form . . . comes with more true novelty than any
book of verse published in England for some years."—*Athenæum.*
    " Some men seem to avoid fame as sedulously as the majority seek it. Mr. Selwyn
Image is one of these. He has achieved a charming fame by his very shyness and
mystery. His very name has a look of having been designed by the Century Guild,
and it was certainly first published in *The Century Guild Hobby Horse.*"—*The Realm.*
    " In the tiny little volume of verse, ' Poems and Carols,' by Selwyn Image,
we discern a note of spontaneous inspiration, a delicate and graceful fancy, and
considerable, but unequal, skill of versification. The Carols are skilful reproductions
of that rather archaic form of composition, devotional in tone and felicitous in
sentiment. Love and nature are the principal themes of the Poems. It is difficult
not to be hackneyed in the treatment of such themes, but Mr. Image successfully
overcomes the difficulty."—*The Times.*
    " The Catholic movement in literature, a strong reality to-day in England as in
France, if working within narrow limits, has its newest interpretation in Mr. Selwyn
Image's ' Poems and Carols.' Of course the book is charming to look at and to
handle, since it is his. The Chiswick Press and Mr. Mathews have helped him to
realize his design."—*The Sketch.*

ISHAM FACSIMILE REPRINTS; Nos. III. and IV.
    See BRETON and SOUTHWELL.
    ** New Elizabethan Literature at the British Museum, see
The Times, 31 August, 1894, also *Notes and Queries,* Sept., 1894.

[By the Author of *The Art of Thomas Hardy*].
JOHNSON (LIONEL).

POEMS. With a title design and colophon by H. P. HORNE.
Printed at the CHISWICK PRESS, on hand-made paper.
Sq. post 8vo. 5*s. net*.
Also, 25 special copies at 15*s. net*.
Boston: Copeland and Day.

"Full of delicate fancy, and display much lyrical grace and felicity."—*Times*.

"An air of solidity, combined with something also of severity, is the first impression one receives from these pages. . . . The poems are more massive than most lyrics are; they aim at dignity and attain it. This is, we believe, the first book of verse that Mr. Johnson has published; and we would say, on a first reading, that for a first book it was remarkably mature. And so it is, in its accomplishment, its reserve of strength, its unfaltering style. . . . Whatever form his writing takes, it will be the expression of a rich mind, and a rare talent."—*Saturday Review*.

"Mr. Lionel Johnson's poems have the advantage of a two-fold inspiration. Many of these austere strains could never have been written if he had not been steeped in the most golden poetry of the Greeks; while, on the other hand, side by side with the mellifluous chanting, there comes another note, mild, sweet, and unsophisticated—the very bird-note of Celtic poetry. And then again one comes on a very ripe and affluent, as of one who has spoiled the very goldenest harvests of song of cultivated ages. . . . Mr. Johnson's poetry is concerned with lofty things and is never less than passionately sincere. It is sane, high-minded, and full of felicities."—*Illustrated London News*.

"The most obvious characteristics of Mr. Johnson's verse are dignity and distinction; but beneath these one feels a passionate poetic impulse, and a grave fascinating music passes from end to end of the volume."—*Realm*.

"It is at once stately and passionate, austere, and free. His passion has a sane mood; his fire a white heat. . . . Once again it is the Celtic spirit that makes for higher things. Mr. Johnson's muse is concerned only with the highest. Her flight is as of a winged thing, that goes 'higher still and higher,' and has few flutterings near earth."—*Irish Daily Independent*.

JOHNSON (EFFIE).

IN THE FIRE, AND OTHER FANCIES. With frontispiece by WALTER CRANE. Imperial 16mo. 3*s. 6d. net*.

LAMB (CHARLES).

BEAUTY AND THE BEAST. With an Introduction by ANDREW LANG. Facsimile Reprint of the rare First Edition. *With 8 choice stipple engravings in brown ink, after the original plates.* Royal 16mo. 3*s. 6d. net*.
Transferred to the present Publisher.

MARSON (REV. C. L.).

A VOLUME OF SHORT STORIES. [*In preparation.*

MARSTON (PHILIP BOURKE).

A LAST HARVEST: LYRICS AND SONNETS FROM THE
BOOK OF LOVE. Edited, with Biographical Sketch,
by LOUISE CHANDLER MOULTON. 500 copies. Printed
by MILLER & SON. Post 8vo. 5s. net.
[*Very few remain.*
Also 50 copies on hand-made L.P. 10s. 6d. net.
[*Very few remain.*

"Among the sonnets with which the volume concludes, there are some fine
examples of a form of verse in which all competent authorities allow that Marston
excelled. 'The Breadth and Beauty of the Spacious Night,' 'To All in Haven,'
'Friendship and Love,' 'Love's Deserted Palace'—these, to mention no others,
have the 'high seriousness' which Matthew Arnold made the test of true poetry."—
Athenæum.
"Mrs. Chandler Moulton's biography is a beautiful piece of writing, and her
estimate of his work—a high estimate—is also a just one."—*Black and White.*

MASON (A. E. W.).

A ROMANCE OF WASTDALE. Crown 8vo. 3s. 6d. net.
[*Immediately.*

MORRISON (G. E.).

ALONZO QUIXANO, otherwise DON QUIXOTE: being a
dramatization of the Novel of CERVANTES, and espe-
cially of those parts which he left unwritten. Cr. 8vo.
1s. net.

MUSA CATHOLICA.

Selected and Edited by MRS. WILLIAM SHARP.
[*In preparation.*

MURRAY (ALMA).

PORTRAIT AS BEATRICE CENCI. With Critical Notice
containing Four Letters from ROBERT BROWNING.
8vo. 2s. net.

NOEL (HON. RODEN).

MY SEA, and other posthumous Poems. With an Intro-
duction by STANLEY ADDLESHAW. [*In preparation.*
SELECTED LYRICS FROM THE WORKS OF THE LATE HON.
RODEN NOEL. With a Biographical and Critical
Essay by PERCY ADDLESHAW. Illustrated with Two
Portraits, including a reproduction of the famous
picture by W. B. RICHMOND, A. [*In preparation.*

NOEL (HON. RODEN)—continued.

POOR PEOPLE'S CHRISTMAS. Printed at the AYLESBURY
PRESS. 250 copies. 16mo. 1s. net.
[Very few remain.

"Displays the author at his best. . . . , Mr. Noel always has something
to say worth saying, and his technique—though like Browning, he is too intent upon
idea to bestow all due care upon form—is generally sufficient and sometimes
masterly. We hear too seldom from a poet of such deep and kindly sympathy."—
Sunday Times.

O'SULLIVAN (VINCENT).

POEMS. With a title-design by SELWYN IMAGE.
[In preparation.

POWELL (F. YORK).

See CORBIN.

PROBYN (MAY).

PANSIES : A BOOK OF POEMS. With a title-page and cover
design by MINNIE MATHEWS. Fcap. 8vo. 3s. 6d. net.

"*De mon jardin, voyageur,*
Vous me demandez une fleur?
Cueillez toujours—mais je n'ai,
Voyageur, que des pensées."

"Miss Probyn's new volume is a slim one, but rare in quality. She is no mere
pretty verse maker; her spontaneity and originality are beyond question, and so far
as colour and picturesqueness go, only Mr. Francis Thompson rivals her among the
English Catholic poets of to-day."—*Sketch.*

"This too small book is a mine of the purest poetry, very holy, and very
refined, and removed as far as possible from the tawdry or the common-place."—*Irish
Monthly.*

"The religious poems are in their way perfect, with a tinge of the mysticism
one looks for in the poetry of two centuries ago, but so seldom meets with nowadays."
—*Catholic Times.*

"Full of a delicate devotional sentiment and much metrical felicity."—*Times.*

RHYMERS' CLUB, THE SECOND BOOK OF THE.

Contributions by E. DOWSON, E. J. ELLIS, G. A. GREENE,
A. HILLIER, LIONEL JOHNSON, RICHARD LE GAL-
LIENNE, VICTOR PLARR, E. RADFORD, E. RHYS,
T. W. ROLLESTONE, ARTHUR SYMONS, J. TOD-
HUNTER, W. B. YEATS. Printed by MILLER & SON.
500 copies (of which 400 are for sale). 16mo. 5s. net.
50 copies on hand-made L.P. 10s. 6d. net.

New York : Dodd, Mead & Co.

"The work of twelve very competent verse writers, many of them not unknown
to fame. This form of publication is not a new departure exactly, but it is a recur-
rence to the excellent fashion of the Elizabethan age, when 'England's Helicon,'

RHYMERS' CLUB, SECOND BOOK OF THE—continued.

Davison's 'Poetical Rhapsody,' and 'Phœnix Nest,' with scores of other collections, contained the best songs of the best song-writers of that tuneful epoch."—*Black and White.*

"The future of these thirteen writers, who have thus banded themselves together, will be watched with interest. Already there is fulfilment in their work, and there is much promise." —*Speaker.*

"In the intervals of Welsh rarebit and stout provided for them at the 'Cheshire Cheese,' in Fleet Street, the members of the Rhymers' Club have produced some very pretty poems, which Mr. Elkin Mathews has issued in his notoriously dainty manner."—*Pall Mall Gazette.*

ROBERTSON-HICKS (MAUDE).
  SPRING VOICES.   [*Shortly.*

ROTHENSTEIN (WILL).
  OCCASIONAL PORTRAITS. With comments on the Personages by various writers.   [*In preparation.*

SCHAFF (DR. P.).
  LITERATURE AND POETRY: Papers on Dante, Latin Hymns, &c.   Portrait and Plates.   100 copies only. 8vo. 10s. net.   [*Very few remain.*

SCULL (W. D.).
  THE GARDEN OF THE MATCHBOXES, and other Stories. Crown 8vo. 3s. 6d. net.   [*In preparation.*

STRANGE (E. F.)
  A BOOK OF THOUGHTS.   [*In preparation.*
          [Isham Facsimile Reprint].

S[OUTHWELL] (R[OBERT]).
  A FOVREFOVLD MEDITATION, OF THE FOURE LAST THINGS. COMPOSED IN A DIUINE POEME. By R. S. The author of S. Peter's complaint. London, 1606. A Facsimile Reprint, with a Bibliographical Note by CHARLES EDMONDS. 150 copies.   Printed on hand-made paper at the CHISWICK PRESS. Roy. 16mo. 5s. net.
  Also 50 copies, large paper. 7s. 6d. net.

  Facsimile reprint from the unique fragment discovered in the autumn of 1867 by Mr. Charles Edmonds in a disused lumber room at Lamport Hall, Northants, and lately purchased by the British Museum authorities. This fragment supplies the first sheet of a previously unknown poem by Robert Southwell, the Roman Catholic poet, whose religious fervour lends a pathetic beauty to everything that he wrote, and future editors of Southwell's works will find it necessary to give it close study. The whole of the Poem has been completed from two MS. copies, which differ in the number of Stanzas.

SYMONDS (JOHN ADDINGTON).

IN THE KEY OF BLUE, AND OTHER PROSE ESSAYS.
With cover designed by C. S. RICKETTS. Printed at
the BALLANTYNE PRESS. Second Edition. Thick
cr. 8vo. 8s. 6d. net.

New York: Macmillan & Co.

"The variety of Mr. Symonds' interests! Here are criticisms upon the Venetian
Tiepolo, upon M. Zola, upon Mediæval Norman Songs, upon Elizabethan lyrics,
upon Plato's and Dante's ideals of love; and not a sign anywhere, except may be in
the last, that he has more concern for, or knowledge of, one theme than another.
Add to these artistic themes the delighted records of English or Italian scenes, with
their rich beauties of nature or of art, and the human passions that inform them.
How joyous a sense of great possessions won at no man's hurt or loss must such a
man retain."—*Daily Chronicle.*

"Some of the essays are very charming, in Mr. Symonds' best style, but the
first one, that which gives its name to the volume, is at least the most curious of the
lot."—*Speaker.*

"The other essays are the work of a sound and sensible critic."—*National
Observer.*

"The literary essays are more restrained, and the prepared student will find them
full of illumination and charm, while the descriptive papers have the attractiveness
which Mr. Symonds always gives to work in this *genre*."—MR. JAS. ASHCROFT
NOBLE, in *The Literary World.*

TENNYSON (LORD).

See HALLAM,—VAN DYKE.

TODHUNTER (DR. JOHN).

A SICILIAN IDYLL. With a Frontispiece by WALTER
CRANE. Printed at the CHISWICK PRESS. 250 copies.
Imp. 16mo. 5s. net. 50 copies hand-made L. P. Fcap.
4to. 10s. 6d. net. [*Very few remain.*

"He combines his notes skilfully, and puts his own voice, so to speak, into
them, and the music that results is sweet and of a pastoral tunefulness."—*Speaker.*

"The blank verse is the true verse of pastoral, quiet and scholarly, with frequent
touches of beauty. The echoes of Theocritus and of the classics at large are modest
and felicitous."—*Anti-Jacobin.*

"A charming little pastoral play in one act. The verse is singularly graceful,
and many bright gems of wit sparkle in the dialogues."—*Literary World.*

"Well worthy of admiration for its grace and delicate finish, its clearness, and
its compactness."—*Athenæum.*

Also the following works by the same Author transferred
to the present Publisher, viz. :—LAURELLA, and other
Poems, 5s. net.—ALCESTIS, a Dramatic Poem, 4s. net.
—A STUDY OF SHELLEY, 5s. 6d. net.—FOREST SONGS,
and other Poems, 3s. net.—THE BANSHEE, 3s. net.—
HELENA IN TROAS, 2s. 6d. net.

TYNAN (KATHARINE).

See HINKSON.

VAN DYKE (HENRY).

THE POETRY OF TENNYSON.   Third Edition, enlarged.
Cr. 8vo.   5s. 6d. *net.*

*The additions consist of a Portrait, Two Chapters, and the
Bibliography expanded.   The Laureate himself gave valuable
aid in correcting various details.*

"Mr. Elkin Mathews publishes a new edition, revised and enlarged, of that
excellent work, 'The Poetry of Tennyson,' by Henry Van Dyke.   The additions
are considerable.   It is extremely interesting to go over the bibliographical notes
to see the contemptuous or, at best, contemptuously patronising tone of the reviewers
in the early thirties gradually turning to civility, to a loud chorus of applause."—
Anti-Jacobin.

"Considered as an aid to the study of the Laureate, this labour of love merits
warm commendation.   Its grouping of the poems, its bibliography and chronology,
its catalogue of Biblical allusion and quotations, are each and all substantial accessories
to the knowledge of the author."—DR. RICHARD GARNETT, in the *Illustrated
London News.*

WATSON (E. H. LACON).

THE UNCONSCIOUS HUMOURIST, AND OTHER ESSAYS.
[*In preparation.*

[*Mr. Wedmore's Short Stories.   New and Uniform Issue.
Crown 8vo., each Volume* 3s. 6d. *net.*]

WEDMORE (FREDERICK).

PASTORALS OF FRANCE.   Fourth Edition.   Crown 8vo.
3s. 6d. *net.* [*Ready.*

New York : Charles Scribner's Sons.

"A writer in whom delicacy of literary touch is united with an almost disem-
bodied fineness of sentiment."—*Athenæum.*

"Of singular quaintness and beauty."—*Contemporary Review.*

"The stories are exquisitely told."—*The World.*

"Delicious idylls, written with Mr. Wedmore's fascinating command of
sympathetic incident, and with his characteristic charm of style."—*Illustrated London
News.*

"The publication of the 'Pastorals' may be said to have revealed, not only a new
talent, but a new literary *genre.* .   The charm of the writing never fails."—*Bookman.*

"In their simplicity, their tenderness, their quietude, their truthfulness to the
remote life that they depict, 'Pastorals of France' are almost perfect."—*Spectator.*

WEDMORE (FREDERICK)—continued.

RENUNCIATIONS. Third Edition. With a Portrait by
J. J. SHANNON. Cr. 8vo. 3s. 6d. net.   [Ready.

New York: Charles Scribner's Sons.

"These are clever studies in polite realism."—*Athenæum.*

"They are quite unusual. The picture of Richard Pelse, with his one moment of romance, is exquisite."—*St. James's Gazette.*

"'The Chemist in the Suburbs,' in 'Renunciations,' is a pure joy. . . . The story of Richard Pelse's life is told with a power not unworthy of the now disabled hand that drew for us the lonely old age of M. Parent."—MR. TRAILL, in *The New Review.*

"The book belongs to the highest order of imaginative work. 'Renunciations' are studies from the life—pictures which make plain to us some of the innermost workings of the heart."—*Academy.*

"Mr. Wedmore has gained for himself an enviable reputation. His style has distinction, has form. He has the poet's secret how to bring out the beauty of common things. . . . 'The Chemist in the Suburbs,' in 'Renunciations,' is his masterpiece."—*Saturday Review.*

"We congratulate Mr. Wedmore on his vivid, wholesome, and artistic work, so full of suppressed feeling and of quiet strength."—*Standard.*

ENGLISH EPISODES. Second Edition. Cr. 8vo. 3s. 6d. net.   [Ready.

New York: Charles Scribner's Sons.

"Distinction is the characteristic of Mr. Wedmore's manner. These things remain on the mind as things seen ; not read of."—*Daily News.*

"A penetrating insight, a fine pathos. Mr. Wedmore is a peculiarly fine and sane and carefully deliberate artist."—*Westminster Gazette.*

"In 'English Episodes' we have another proof of Mr. Wedmore's unique position among the writers of fiction of the day. We hardly think of his short volumes as 'stories,' but rather as life-secrets and hearts' blood, crystallised somehow, and, in their jewel-form, cut with exceeding skill by the hand of a master-workman. . . The faultless episode of the 'Vicar of Pimlico' is the best in loftiness of purpose and keenness of interest; but the 'Fitting Obsequies' is in equal on different lines, and deserves to be a classic."—*World.*

"'English Episodes' are worthy successors of 'Pastorals' and 'Renunciations,' and with them should represent a permanent addition to Literature."—*Academy.*

There may also be had the Collected Edition (1893) of "Pastorals of France" and "Renunciations," with Title-page by John Fulleylove, R.I. 5s. net.

WICKSTEED (P. H., Warden of University Hall).

DANTE : SIX SERMONS.

. A FOURTH EDITION. (Unaltered Reprint). Cr. 8vo. 2s. net.

"It is impossible not to be struck with the reality and earnestness with which Mr. Wicksteed seeks to do justice to what are the supreme elements of the *Commedia*, its spiritual significance, and the depth and insight of its moral teaching."—*Guardian.*

WYNNE (FRANCES).

WHISPER! A Volume of Verse. Fcap. 8vo. buckram.
2s. 6d. net.

Transferred by the Author to the present Publisher.

" A little volume of singularly sweet and graceful poems, hardly one of which
can be read by any lover of poetry without definite pleasure, and everyone who reads
either of them without is, we venture to say, unable to appreciate that play of light
and shadow on the heart of man which is of the very essence of poetry."—*Spectator.*

" The book includes, to my humble taste, many very charming pieces, musical,
simple, straightforward and *not* 'as sad as night.' It is long since I have read a more
agreeable volume of verse, successful up to the measure of its aims and ambitions."—
MR. ANDREW LANG, in *Longman's Magazine.*

YEATS (W. B.).

THE SHADOWY WATERS. A Poetic Play. [*In preparation.*

THE WIND AMONG THE REEDS (Poems). [*In preparation.*

MR. ELKIN MATHEWS *holds likewise the only copies of the
following Books printed at the Private Press of the* REV.
C. HENRY DANIEL, *Fellow of Worcester College, Oxford.*

BRIDGES (ROBERT).

THE GROWTH OF LOVE. Printed in Fell's old English
type, on Whatman paper. 100 copies. Fcap. 4to.
£2. 12s. 6d. net.

SHORTER POEMS. Printed in Fell's old English type, on
Whatman paper. 100 copies. Five Parts. Fcap. 4to.
£2. 12s. 6d. net.   [*Very few remain.*

HYMNI ECCLESIÆ CVRA HENRICI DANIEL.

Small 8vo. (1882), £1. 15s. net.

BLAKE HIS SONGS OF INNOCENCE

Sq. 16mo. 100 copies only. 12s. 6d. net.

MILTON ODE ON THE NATIVITY.

Sq. 16mo. 10s. 6d. net.